Copyright © 2025 by Sunsational Publishing, LLC

ISBN 978-1-953416-31-5

All rights reserved.
No part of this publication may be reproduced, distributed, or transmitted in any form or by any means, including photocopying, recording, or other electronic or mechanical methods, without the prior written permission of the publisher, except in the case of brief quotations embodied in critical reviews and certain other noncommercial uses permitted by copyright law.

Other works by Janet Hogan Chapman:
Madam May: A tale of madams, morphine, moonshine, and murder

After Madam May

Dorothy May: Can she find a forever family?

MotherLove

This teacher talks:
What really goes on in America's schools, a memoir

Acknowledgement

I want to acknowledge several people who have contributed to making this book a reality. Thank you, family, friends, and writing colleagues who provided valuable feedback throughout the writing process and listened to me ramble on about these characters. Thank you to my new friend and publisher, Theresa D. Berger of Sunsational Publishing LLC, for working with me to get this book published. Your advice, accessibility, and expertise were all appreciated. Thanks also to the editor, Amy Shook, for catching my faux pas and working on a tight schedule. A very special, big thanks to Red Maylon, book designer and illustrator, for her formatting skills and especially for the gorgeous cover. These women have all helped me fulfill my mission as GeorgiaJanet – to empower strong women through the written word. May you all feel empowered for being a part of this project.

Janet Hogan Chapman
aka GeorgiaJanet,
"The Bohemian Southern Belle"
www.georgiajanet.com

This book is dedicated
to all those who came before
and those who will come after.

AUTHOR'S NOTE

The characters portrayed in this book are real.
The content is mostly based on real events.
The letters have been fictionalized based on context.
In reality, the letter box and letters do not exist.
The reflections and the letters to my granddaughters
are my own and are genuine expressions.
The following are my maternal ancestors,
who are the main characters in the book.

My Great-Great-Grandmother
Margaret Adaline Parks Howell (Clark F.)
1843-1936

Her oldest child, my Great-Grandmother
Harriet Lucille Howell Smith (William B.)
1864-1929

Her youngest daughter, my Grandmother
Tommie Belle Smith Lord (Clarence J.)
1899-1961

Her youngest daughter, my Mother
Mary Elizabeth Lord Holliday Hogan
(Boyce W., James F.)
1923-2000

Her youngest daughter, Myself
Janet Marie Hogan Chapman (Joseph G.)
1953-

I had no daughters. My six Granddaughters are:
McKenzie 2002-
Macie 2004-
Mabrie 2010-
Savannah 2011-
Cali 2014-
Bailey 2020-

The Letter Box

Janet Hogan Chapman

Introduction

I am no one's daughter. At least I haven't felt like anyone's daughter for many years. My parents passed decades ago. Technically, I suppose I am still their daughter, just not in an alive sense. I wish I had known my mother and the grandmothers who came before her. I mean, really known them, as women. All of them, unlike myself, became mothers to daughters. Adeline, Harriet, Tommie Belle, and finally Mary, who was mother to me. The mother-to-daughter progression ended there, as I had no daughters.

Who were these women? What were their thoughts, dreams, desires, and burdens? I knew they had lived through wars, pestilence, stillbirths, deaths of children, deaths of husbands, back-breaking farm or factory labor, and poverty, all while enduring the civil and societal restraints levied upon women during each of their lives. Still, I did not truly know them.

Until I found the letter box. A faded floral-print box hidden away in some of my mother's old belongings. Inside were packets of letters bound in time-paled ribbons. As I began to unfold and read the brittle pages, it became clear there was a specific order in these epistles from the past. The first was a letter from my great-great-grandmother, Adeline Park Howell, to her daughter, Harriet Howell Smith. The letters in the box would reveal the lives of the women I so longed to know. And, no matter how many years had passed, we were inextricably connected.

PART ONE

ADELINE, MY GREAT-GREAT-GRANDMOTHER, AND HARRIET

HARRIET WRITES TO HER MOTHER, ADELINE, IN RESPONSE TO LEARNING OF HER FATHER, CLARK'S, DEATH

Gainesville, Georgia
July 1903

Dear Mother,

I hope this letter finds you well. It has been quite some time since we corresponded, except for the short telegram regarding Father's death. I am sorry I could not make it out there for services. As for me, I have not been in very good spirits. Since the news of Father's death, I have been somewhat preoccupied with matters of serious concern. Your letter sent me into a turmoil of memories and raised many questions in my heart and soul. I have no answers to these disturbing questions. I feel that I barely knew my father, having been left in the care of his parents when I was very young during his many endeavors to establish a gainful living, both in Georgia then in Texas. Truly, Grandfather Hampton and Grandmother Cynthia were more like my mother and father than either you or my actual father.

I know it was hard times back in those days. However, especially now, being a mother myself, I cannot fathom abandoning a child at such a tender age. It causes my heart to hurt to think that you and Father could have cared so little for me and for my little brother Wade, too. Why could you not send for us? Why is it that all the other children eventually ended up in Texas with you and Father? We were like two foundlings, always aware we were not truly at home with our Grandparents. Oh, they provided well for us and were loving, never cruel. Still, somehow, we always knew we were visitors not permanently installed in their gracious home.

Father's passing and my thoughts of family have made me long for a visit with you. It's been years since we have talked in person. We have

never had the opportunity to talk about my early years, and I would love to hear your thoughts. It may not be too late for us to rekindle a mother-daughter bond. Perhaps one day, I will make it to Texas, but family priorities prohibit me from making such a trip at this time.
I will not leave my children as you did.

As you know, my youngest daughter and son, Tommie and Ernest, are still just three and one years of age. My oldest, Addie, is engaged to be married this November. Daisy, the next oldest, married this past April. Howell, Pugh, Charlie, Bessie, and Maude are all home, of course. I still grieve for my little Park, who lived only a few hours. He would be two now. I'm sure you understand a mother's grief having lost little Wiley at such a young age, even though you have much company out there with all my younger sisters' and brother Parks' families so close by. They are fortunate to have their mother near now that Father is gone.

I look forward to your letters with much anticipation, although, of course, they are much too far and few between.

I do hope to hear from you soon.

Your loving eldest child,

Harriet Smith

Jonesboro, Texas
September 1903

Dear Daughter,

My darling Harriet, my firstborn daughter, how can I begin to explain? Your recent letter caused me much distress. I never suspected you harbored such feelings of resentment and anger towards your father and me at leaving you and your brother behind in Georgia when we moved to Texas. With your father's passing last May, it has been difficult for me to face so much heartache. Perhaps if you could have made your way out to Texas, we could have overcome some of your bitterness and alleviated some of my own despair. To say that news of your father's death sent you into a turmoil of memories stung me in the heart. When you went on to say Grandfather Hampton and Grandmother Cynthia were more like a mother and father to you and your younger brother Wade than either I or your actual father, my mother's heart was broken. I had no idea you harbored such rancor after all these years. It does explain your determination not to leave your own children on their own to visit your family when your father died. I am still greatly despondent and, most of the time, do not know how I will go on.

I am sorry. I know there is no excuse, but I will try to explain – not that any explanation can justify our actions. I don't expect you to understand, and it may take many letters for me to tell the tale. My hands are old and frail, and I can only write so much at a time. Please be patient with me. I will write again soon and pray that you can find it in your heart to grant me forgiveness for my unintended mistakes.

Your Mother,

Adeline Park Howell

Jonesboro, Texas
September 1903

Dear Harriet,

First, I would like to tell you about the beginning of your life. It was such a tumultuous time. You came into this world in February of 1864, well before the end of the devastating War of the Rebellion. Thankfully, your father returned unscathed, but the land, family wealth, and spirits of our families were perilously endangered. I cannot tell you how much I missed you the first time you were taken away from me. Your birth was harrowing, and my physician father insisted I remain under his care. Before I knew what had happened, your grandfather and grandmother Howell whisked you away. I knew they had fared better during the war over in Milton County than my own family had in Greene, but that did not mean I would not provide any less love or sustenance for you. Yet, I was coerced into letting you go. It helped a bit that your father was trying to carve out a living for us adjacent to his father's land, and I knew he would be in their household with you.

our father, Clark, would bring you to visit every other week or so, and you grew into an enchanting babe, but it was clear from your constant crying that you were not familiar with me or my parents. It took about a year for your father to have our home ready in Milton, and finally, I was able to join him there and become your mother in a real sense. Unfortunately, the damage was done. You preferred the company of the elder Howells and spent as much time at their home as you did your own. When your little brother, Wade, was born just two years later, it was a comparable situation. I know Grandmother Cynthia had hoped for a large family, but when Clark's difficult birth and Hampton's subsequent indiscretions made it plain your father, Clark, would be their only child, she was left to fulfill her desire for doting on little ones with her grandchildren. In that regard, you and Wade were showered with affection and material goods.

Harriet, you are a grown woman with life's burdens of your own, and I know you will not mind my speaking so frankly with you about family matters. I tire so easily now that your father has passed on, and it falls on your younger sisters and me to keep the farm going and see that the cattle are cared for. I do not know how much longer we shall be able to maintain our small property. There is much more I need to tell you so I will attempt to write again soon. It is a long story, and it will take time to put it all into words.

Your loving Mother,

Adeline Park Howell

Jonesboro, Texas
November 1903

Dear Daughter,

I hope you and your children are well. I know it is not an easy life raising such a large brood. All my children, though mostly grown, and my many grandchildren keep me well-occupied. I am puzzled at your lack of response to my letters so far, particularly since you were the one who reached out to me. I hope you are still not so cross with me. I shall continue to write to you, as there is much I want you to know and understand. I believe it may be helpful for you to understand the time before the war came to Georgia before you were born. I want to tell you in detail how your father and I came to fall in love. Yes, I was once a young woman, your father was once a young man, and we had hopes and dreams for a beautiful life together, much like the life to which we were accustomed. Alas, as the story is told, you will know that was not to be the case.

Real life for me was nearly perfect in those halcyon days before war. By the time I was born in 1843, the Indian threat was nearly non-existent if one didn't venture too far West. Picnics by the river were grand affairs in summertime. Lavish spreads of cold meats, bread, cheese, and fruit prepared by what we thought were the loving hands of the kitchen help. Baskets packed and carried on the backs of slaves who we were sure lived just to serve our every need. We young ladies tried to sneak downstream, avoiding the hawk eyes of our mammies so that we could remove our slippers and dip our feet into the cool water. We knew they would be preoccupied watching the younger brothers, sisters, and cousins.

My mammy had practically raised me and my older sisters. Now, she had the care of my younger sister and little brothers, too. My mother was only fifteen when she married my father, and as usual, every three years, another child came along. There was always an assortment of cousins, too, so one or two other mammies would be enlisted to supervise. No doubt our mothers were content to have an afternoon of peace, knowing their children were well cared for.

Among other duties, the mammies were there to be sure no young gentlemen would happen along and find us unchaperoned. They ensured we had a proper afternoon rest in the shade, watching that we didn't frolic in the sun and spoil our milk-white complexions. They saw to it that our voluminous skirts and hoops stayed on the quilts so they did not get grass-stained. I'm sure they would have fought off vicious wildlife to protect our very lives if it came down to it.

Fall came late to that part of Georgia. It never failed to delight with cooler days, chilly nights, and brilliant fire-like colors painting the woods. The snow-white fields of cotton were picked clean, and only sad little tufts left here and there bore evidence of the hours of back-breaking picking by bleeding rag-wrapped hands of slaves. It would be years before I realized the injustice of that system. We were elated the harvest was in, and the celebrations of wealth could commence.

Our Greene County barbecues were renowned. Friends, relatives, and other families traveled to one plantation or another each weekend, often staying overnight. All were happy to share the fruits of the labors of "their people." Men showed off their land and livestock, while women showed off the sumptuous food prepared by the kitchen help and their darling youngest children, who were trotted out for display by mammies before being trundled off to bed.

Greeting, flirting, and polite conversation took the better part of the afternoon as guests arrived from near and far. I stood near Father, the better to eye the young men arriving. That's when I was introduced to your father, a dashing young man on a fine steed. We engaged in pleasantries, then reluctantly parted. I say reluctantly because the first moment we looked into each other's eyes, the spell was cast. As custom dictated, we each had to go our separate ways, but in the following hours of frivolity and food, we each caught the other in curious but thoughtful glances across and around those who tried to command our attention. It was as if we sent silent sentiments through the air. Later. We can be together later.

The sky flamed pink, purple, and orange as the sun set. Small knots of young ladies and gentlemen edged away from the raucous men and bustling women, setting their sights on the fair maiden or dashing young man with whom they hoped to share their supper, then dances, and even a stolen kiss before the evening was over.

The smoky scent of pork and beef roasting on spits over open pits saturated the air. Long boards set on upturned log sections sagged with the weight of every imaginable food hot from ovens at the back of the big house. China, silver, and glassware had all been polished and laid out for the feast. My father, or the owner of whatever other plantation happened to be hosting, would climb up on a chair and get everyone's attention with his booming voice as a hush fell over the crowd.

"I want to welcome you all to our humble home; without friends and family, a man is poor indeed. So please, take your fill and enjoy this evening of fellowship. Now, let us thank the Lord for our blessings.

"Dear Lord, we thank thee for these and all our other blessings. Thank you for granting us a bountiful harvest, good health, and peaceful lives. We beseech you to keep us in this contented state for generations to come. Amen."

Laudatory amens rumbled as the men made their way to the serving board or roasting pits. Maids heaped steaming food onto plates. Fried chicken, greens, peas, squash, and beans of every hue. Hot bread dripping with butter was set atop the sides. For men who went to the roasting pits first, all this was laid over slabs of succulent meat cut right off the spit. If they came to the serving board first, the thick cuts of flesh covered the heaping piles already spooned onto the plates. After the men settled down, the women had their turn.

Befitting their modest and dainty demeanor, there was a marked difference in the food gracing ladies' plates. Perhaps one or two spoons of a vegetable, a small slice of chicken breast, and, if they felt especially indulgent, a tiny roll or square of cornbread. Maids made even smaller plates for the children. Some ladies sat, but many ended up standing as they nibbled.

A quiet murmur fell over the grounds as conversation gave way to enjoying the food. Some men went back for more, knowing the maids would be clearing the serving table to make way for the crowning glory of cakes, pies, and confections that were soon to follow. Once that exchange took place, the young and older men's plates would once again be piled high. The ladies and young females would not indulge. They needed to avoid anything that might make the voluminous dancing gowns into which they would be changing too tight for comfort. They drifted from the yard into the big house, glancing over their shoulders at certain young men they hoped to entertain later. Children tried to sneak handfuls of sweets into pockets and under shifts before their nursemaids whisked them away for bedtime.

The men ambled off to smoke, drink, and even make a few gentlemen's agreements. The animals had been settled into shelters with fresh hay and water. The women and young ladies had disappeared into the house, and children were out of sight. Only a few darkies were left about, scurrying back and forth to get the food put away, the dishes to the kitchen, furniture returned to the house, and the considerable amount of waste cleared away. Two old men-servants who could barely walk anymore took up posts tending the fire pits to make sure no embers escaped. Yard dogs made quick work of anything edible on the ground. A few feral cats joined them, keeping a safe distance. Their presence would keep rats, field mice, and other rodents from being attracted to any food bits left about.

An eerie near silence fell over the darkened grounds. A loud guffaw would emerge from the barnyard occasionally, or a trill of laughter might suddenly flutter out on the air as the door to the big house opened, but for the most part, the atmosphere might fool one into thinking the celebration was over and the satiated plantation denizens were settling down for a night of complacent sleep. Ah, but that was not the case. If you'd ever attended one of these barbecues, you would know differently.

Oh, Harriet, those days seem so long ago, and indeed, they were a lifetime ago for so many. This letter has been long and difficult to write. I daresay this remembrance has brought tears to my eyes. I miss your father. I am tired and will have to continue the story in my next letter.

Your Mother,

Adeline Park Howell

Jonesboro, Texas
November 1903

Dear Daughter,

We celebrated a meager Thanksgiving here in our small town. We have enough to keep us fed and sheltered, but I fear my days on this little farm are nearing their end. I cannot go on maintaining a life here as your sisters marry off. I will be forced to sell off whatever I can and make my home elsewhere. Life goes on.

I don't think I got to finish telling you in the last letter about meeting your father. I believe I was describing the lavish barbecues we used to have back on the plantation. The food was stupendous, but for the young folks, it was the events after dinner that we relished. Among the young ladies and gentlemen, the most important and intense part of the event was about to commence. Inside the big house, another transformation had taken place. Throughout the downstairs rooms, furniture had been pushed back along the walls, and rugs had been rolled away. A few small tables here and there boasted refreshments. At one end of the big front parlor, musicians were uncasing instruments, and little bits and pieces of tuning notes flittered out like the chirps of a lost baby bird. If you were a young lady or gentleman of courting age, the tension was building.

Mothers, aunts, and grandmothers gathered in the parlor, anxiously awaiting the beginning of what was a mating ritual. Young men filled the front hall, eyes glued to the curves of the descending staircase in anticipation of entirely different types of curves that would soon come into view. The plantation owner's wife, as presiding First Lady over this event and, in this case, my own Mother, appeared on the top stair landing. A collective gasp of excitement arose from the young gentleman gathered below. Looking down and surveying her domain, my Mother raised her hand, and the signal was passed to the orchestra. The enchanting melody of a waltz emerged. Mother stepped aside. The young women, in their luscious gowns, began to wind down the curving staircase.

My eyes searched the assemblage of young men below. Many returned my gaze, but I moved on fleetingly, not wanting to linger until I found that one set of striking blue eyes. Ah! There he was. The tall, raven-haired young gentleman who boasted the blue eyes hung near the back of the group, leaning casually against the front door frame, a tumbler of whiskey in his right hand.

The time had come, and later, it had arrived. I led the procession of belles. When I stepped onto the marbled floor of the foyer, the gentlemen surged forward, and the belles behind me dispersed into the anxious tide of young men. I did not let them hold me back. Like a stream making its way around stones, I moved forward deliberately, winding my way toward Mr. Clark Forsythe Howell. We stood facing each other, speechless. He slowly raised his glass and swallowed a healthy gulp of the clear home brew. His eyes never left mine when he placed the emptied tumbler on a small table nearby. He reached for my hand.

He bowed, taking my hand and placing a lingering kiss on the back of my satin-gloved hand. As my skin flushed and my heart raced, I was nearly swept away. I came to my senses enough to glance around nervously. Such a blatant display of affection was not considered appropriate! Mr. Howell smiled.

"Don't fret, Miss Park. I took care to wait until the others moved away. No one saw my boorish indiscretion."

I blushed further. Suddenly, I realized my hand was still held firmly in his. I removed it abruptly.

A frown wrinkled his forehead. "Perhaps I should apologize? Was I mistaken? I genuinely believed you enjoyed receiving my forwardness as much as I enjoyed bestowing it."

The blush now covered all my exposed complexion, giving away any pretense I might raise of denying my enjoyment. "Mr. Howell, my enjoyment, or lack thereof, is not an open topic for discussion. Let us go in and join the dancing."

Thus began my love affair with your father.

My dear, I fear I must stop writing now; my hand tires. Please do not think badly of me for not continuing. There is so much more I want you to know, and as you have reminded me, letters are our only way of sharing thoughts for the time being. I promise to write again soon with more of the story.

Your Mother,

Adeline

Jonesboro, Texas
December 1903

Dear Harriet,

I've not had a letter from you in response to the last several I have written. Writing such long treatises is not an easy task for me, yet I am determined that you shall have knowledge of our lives since you feel you were so excluded while these encounters were taking place. Christmas is approaching, and your little nieces and nephews are growing excited, as I must assume your children are, too. This shall be my first Christmas without your father, and I am growing nostalgic for the past. I shall tell you a little about my own father.

I am certain you know little about him, as he did not have the same level of familiarity with you and Wade as did the Howells. You do kno he was a physician, as I've told you before. The Park family was quite prominent in Greene County. They were interchangeably referred to as "Park" and "Parks." I use the singular version for the sake of expediency. He was truly a remarkable man. He has only been gone since 1895, and I missed him terribly after we relocated to Texas. Thinking of my fondness for him helps me realize how you must have missed the closeness of a father. I do hope Hampton Howell served well in Clark's stead.

There is a conversation I recall that illustrates the wisdom of your Grandfather Park. It was around Eastertime, before the war began when my father summoned me to his study. By that time, Clark and I were secretly certain we would betroth when the time was right, and I, of course, was hoping sooner rather than later. The conversation, as close as I can recall, went something like this.

"Come in, daughter."

"Yes, Father? You wanted to see me?"

"Don't I always want to see my favorite girl child?"

I smiled and swished my big hoop skirt. "Well, I suppose that could be true. But it's unusual to call me in to see you in the middle of the morning. You're usually out tending to animals or people, not taking your leisure here at home."

"Indeed, my girl. I dare say you know my routines well. Though you may not realize it, I know yours just as well, too. Have a seat, daughter. We need to talk."

I arranged myself on the side chair. Those damned hoop skirts were such a bother. Father pulled his chair from behind the desk to sit directly in front of me and took my hands in his. I was apprehensive and silent. Being called to my father's study meant something serious was afoot. I attempted to lighten the mood, and although I grinned, it was no use. "Oh Father, you know I cherish our talks, but surely you have more pressing matters to attend. Please don't let me keep you..."

Father, the venerable Columbus Monroe Parks, sighed and sat back. Little did either of us know that by this stage of his life when he should be able to slow down and enjoy his family, his farming, and the pleasures of wealth he had managed to accumulate, life as he knew it was about to crumble beneath his very feet like dry Georgia clay during a drought.

"My dear Adeline, that is exactly what I wanted to talk about. There are pressing matters we need to address. I know you are far beyond the intelligence of most girls your age. You must know that with Lincoln in office now and more states seceding from the Union, we are on the brink of war. It's only a matter of time until..."

I did not like the direction our conversation was heading and shook my curls in vehement denial. "Oh, Father, that's silly. I'm sure Mr. Lincoln and Mr. Davis will work out something. It's ridiculous to think there will be an actual war just because we own and need slaves. We treat our people well. What on earth would they do without us? Besides, even if we did have a war, our men would give those Yanks what for, and it'd be over in just a few days, and then we could get back to our lives."

"Oh darling, if only it were that easy. I know we treat our people well, but that's not true of all owners. The idea of owning a person has never sat well with me, but that's our way of life here. If slavery is abolished, as I feel certain it will, our way of life will change. It will never be the same."

My face melted into furrows of concern. It was all I could do to keep my chin from trembling. 'But Father, you don't mean..."

Father leaned closer. "What I mean, dear daughter, is this. We need to be prepared for the worst. Your two older sisters don't appear to have any prospects; your brothers are young yet, and I am too old to fight. With our help gone, we'll be doing well to feed ourselves."

"Oh, Father! We can all work. We won't starve. I'm sure we will find a way to manage."

Father smiled at me indulgently. 'Adeline, I don't doubt for a moment that you will manage just fine. I'm not blind nor so long removed from youth that I don't see the affection growing between you and young Mr. Howell. He will make a fine match. I know him to be a dutiful citizen, as is his entire family. No doubt he will be enlisting when the time comes for that. It would comfort me to know that at least one of my daughters will secure a husband and home of her own when the war ends. There may not be much left here for the others."

Seeing the heavy concern in Father's eyes, my heart was torn. He was truly burdened with the future of his family. I was only slightly embarrassed that he had divined the nature of my and your father's relationship. We had taken advantage of every chance to see each other and wrote letters copiously when we couldn't. We had grown so close to the point of using first names and discussing a future together. Still, the possibility of war had not entered those conversations. Now, I worried Clark may have been avoiding the topic. Would he keep that from me, not wanting to cause distress? This talk with Father led me to realize war was inevitable. Best we address it sooner than later.

I'm sure Father could tell I was disturbed by our conversation. "Adeline, I fear I have saddened your heart with this tedious talk, but you are my single confidante. Your sisters are too silly, your brothers too young, your mother too fragile. The men hereabouts are full of bravado for now, but that will fade soon enough. I pin my hopes on you and young Mr. Howell. Both families are hard-working and industrious and not without resources. That will bode well for whatever lies ahead." Father stood up, pulled me to my feet, and embraced me fiercely. I was so moved by his confidence that tears streamed down my cheeks. "Oh Father, I, I mean we, Clark and I, won't disappoint you."

"I know, I know. That's precisely why we needed to have this talk."

Father pulled out a pressed white handkerchief and patted my cheeks. "There now, daughter, dry your tears. Let's get on to living this life we have now while we still have it."

Harriet, I do hope this glimpse into the nature of your grandfather has been well received. I did love him so much and now regret that you were denied the opportunity to know him and your own father so well. What is done is done. In my next letter I shall tell you more about your own father. Hopefully, it will provide a window into his own gentle nature and desire to protect those he loved.

I do hope you will write soon. However, I realize it may be difficult for you to put your feelings to paper, especially if you still harbor animosity regarding your early upbringing. Do not fret, for I will continue my ramblings in hopes of generating a loving mother-daughter relationship, even at this late stage of our lives.

I wish you all a happy Christmas.

Your loving and regretful Mother,

Adeline Howell

Jonesboro, Texas
January 1904

Dear Harriet,

The weather here in Texas has turned cold, and we've had ice and snow. It is difficult to get out and do chores, and it makes one want to be an indolent soul. We only accomplish the absolute necessities. I have little help since your father is gone. Your brother Park and sisters do what they can, but it is not near enough. I never hear from your other brother, Wade. I assume he is still somewhere in Alabama, but I couldn't say for sure. I hope your family is well and had a joyful Christmas. I had hoped to at least receive a Christmas greeting from you. I know providing for such a large family is a great task; perhaps you were too occupied with family matters.

I believe I left off in the last letter telling you about my father and his concerns about the coming war. Of course, as a youthful optimist, I wasn't convinced it would come to pass. As it turned out, the same day Father talked with me, your own father was due to arrive for a visit. I hung about the house that day, with an ear out for approaching hoofbeats signaling my sweetheart was drawing near.

Finally, my vigilance was rewarded. I hung behind a curtain to catch sight of Clark and heard his greeting as he turned over the reins of his horse and addressed our favored servant, Cyrus.

"Howdy Cyrus, how are you doing this fine morning?"

"I's good, Mr. Howell, I's good. And yourself?"

"Oh, I'm good too, Cyrus. Looking forward to some of that delicious cooking y'all do out here, and of course, I'm anxious to see Miss Parks."

"I knows that's so, Mr. Howell. I 'magine she feels the same. But Mr. Parks, he say send you right to his study. We better do what the massa says."

I could hear the touch of concern in Clark's voice. "Is that right, Cyrus? Well now, I wouldn't be wanting to cause you any trouble with massa Parks, so I better mind what he says. I'll go straight there."

"That's good, Mr. Howell. I'll take care of yo' horse and call y'all when that good food's on the table."

"You do that, Cyrus, you do that."

I dashed from my parlor window post to the dark corner under the staircase, knowing Clark would not be able to see me there, and if, by chance, the study door was left ajar, I would be able to hear their conversation. Father had not said anything to me earlier that morning about needing to speak with Clark, so I was intrigued. I peeked as Clark strode into the house, doffed his hat, and smoothed his unruly hair back off his forehead. He was unaware I was watching from my hiding spot, hoping he would look around for me. Instead, he turned purposefully to the door leading into Father's study. At his polite knock, Father's voice came through clearly.

"Come in, Mr. Howell. I've been expecting you."

Clark disappeared into the study, pulling the door closed behind him. As old doors were wont to do, the door did not catch, and it slowly eased open. I would be able to hear! I could only picture the scene and the looks on their faces, but I could clearly hear their discourse. Considering my own talk with Father earlier, I was apprehensive about what he might want to discuss with Clark. I didn't have long to wait until Father began the conversation.

"Let's sit here where we can talk comfortably. Can I get you anything? It may be a tad early for a whiskey, but it's right here if you'd like some."

"Oh, no, sir, I'm just fine. I'll wait for some of that mint tea y'all serve with luncheon. That will suit me."

"Good choice, young man. I'll wait for that, too. It's a fine early spring day, isn't it? I trust your ride was not too arduous."

"It is a fine day, Mr. Parks and my ride was most invigorating. Not arduous at all."

I made out a low chuckle from Father. "I'm sure it would be for a healthy young man like yourself. Just a casual morning ride from your place over to ours. I have some thoughts I want to discuss with you, but first, you're the one who requested to see me. I have my suspicions, but what exactly is it on your mind? Let's get right down to it."

I was puzzled now. I had no idea that Clark had requested to speak with Father. This was a revelation.

Clark cleared his throat. "Well, uh, Mr. Parks, I wanted to ask you, um, that is to say, uh . . ."

Father interrupted. "Come on, boy, spit it out! It's about my daughter, Adeline, isn't it?"

"Yes, sir, it is."

"Well, go on then, man. What about Adeline?"

"I want to marry her, sir. I love Adeline and I'm asking for her hand in marriage."

I gasped so loudly that I was afraid I would give myself away. I had no idea this was coming.

Well dear, this seems as good a place as any to stop for now. There are chores that I need to attend to before dark falls. I dread going out in the cold, but it must be done. I shall write again and continue the story.

Please do write if you can make time for your old, widowed mother.

Regards,

Adeline Howell

Jonesboro, Texas
February 1904

Dear Harriet,

I must express my disappointment that I have yet to receive any response to my letters. Are you that bitter towards me that you would punish me with no communication? Could you be so busy you cannot spare a moment to reply to your mother as I painfully recall the story of your father and me to enlighten you on the circumstances of your youth? I am determined to inform you about that past. You may or may not be receptive, but I feel it is important that the story be told. Well, enough of that.

I know I left off hearing Clark ask my father for my hand in marriage. Years later, after the war was over, Clark would confide to me how heavy his heart was that very day. He said he knew I was everything he could want in a wife and mother of his children. He knew we both held equal stations in life, me the daughter of a well-off farmer physician. He was the son of an industrious farmer and businessman, and both of us had bloodlines going back to the very founding of the country. Despite that, he already had concerns about the coming war. He told me how some folks tended to brush off Georgia's secession as just a passing thing, thinking that the crisis born of Lincoln's election would be short-lived. Yet there was an undercurrent of unrest throughout northeast Georgia. Like many educated men of his class, Clark suspected that the threat of a war to protect the solidarity of the Union was not just for show. He, his father, and his grandfather before him owned slaves, just like in my own family. Clark admitted to me that he had never questioned the morality of such, accepting it as their way of life. But once the question of slavery was front and center in the face of the coming war, he gave it a great deal of thought. It didn't sit comfortably with him, yet he questioned how they could go on without the labor provided by slaves. Could former owners afford to free them and pay them to stay on? Would they still expect lodging, medical care, and food to be provided? Clark confessed he just couldn't imagine how it could all work out.

Your father went on to tell me that aside from the slavery issue, he was incensed that far-off northerners thought they could dictate what was done in his own home state and other southern states. He felt strange not to be considered part of the Union, but damn, who did Abe Lincoln think he was trying to tell them what they could or could not do down here in Georgia? He reminisced about these thoughts that troubled his mind as he rode to speak with my father that day.

Of course, we had serious conversations before we married. Lincoln had been elected in November of 1860, and Georgia had seceded the following January. Fort Sumter had been fired upon in early April, and we knew then the possibility of war was inevitable. We became officially engaged in late April 1861. At least once a month, Clark would ride out to Greenville and stay a few days at the Park Inn; other times, my sister Betsy and I would journey to the senior Howells' plantation in Gwinnett County. Of course, as a matter of propriety, we were always accompanied by one of our elder male Park cousins. The senior Howells, Clark's parents, Hampton and Cynthia, were delighted to have us young ladies as guests. Clark's absences, being their only child, left them lonely.

During these extended visits, we had plenty to talk about. It was the custom to make decisions about where we would live, business matters, furnishings, household utensils, and supplies, all well before an actual wedding took place. I recall one time, as we talked about these necessities, I sensed hesitancy in Clark's demeanor. We had not set a date and that alone left me more than a trifle anxious. I knew the war weighed on his mind, but it still seemed far away and remote from our lives in Georgia. It was not until years later that he professed those earlier thoughts that I understood.

At the time we were some distance from any actual battle or fighting. After the initial firing on Fort Sumter in South Carolina, it was feared the Union would make an advance westward, coming straight into Georgia, but that did not happen. In April, Lincoln had issued his first proclamation of war, Virginia seceded from the Union, and Robert E. Lee resigned his commission in the United States Army. The stage was set for a lengthy confrontation. By summer, the battles had begun. The Rebels were cheerful and encouraged at their initial successes. We felt no guilt for Clark to wait things out a bit and see what transpired.

I had hoped postponing his enlistment would lighten Clark's mood and inspire him to move forward and set a date for the wedding. I decided to broach the subject one sweltering summer afternoon during one of my visits to the Howells. We sat on a cool stone in the shade of a tree overhanging the western side of the Chattahoochee River near Warsaw. On the far eastern bank of the river was Clark's grandfather, Evan Howell's, adjoining land. I felt emboldened by the vast expanses of land the Howells owned, combined with all the Park property in Greene, Monroe, and Morgan Counties.

Twirling a long, thin, willow branch in the water below, I spoke up. "Clark, dearest, I hear the news from the north is quite in our favor. Is that not indeed so?"

Hesitating before answering, Clark stared into the swirling eddies.

"Well, my darling, some of the news is indeed encouraging. The Union forces have taken a beating so far. Yet I fear it is too soon to hope providence will always be so good. Much is at stake, and we know not what the future will hold. Lincoln's blockade will eventually take a toll, and winter is coming."

I let the branch I was twirling sink into the water and placed my hand on Clark's forearm. "But Clark, surely the war will be concluded by true winter! No one, Union or Rebel, wants to face those weather conditions without the comforts of hearth, home, food, and family. Even men wishing to display their bravery will see the sense in that. Don't you agree?"

He placed his hand on my cheek. Such intimate gestures thrilled me and led my heart to beat as if it would jump out of my chest.

"Oh, my dear, have you not observed your young brothers play-fighting

and seen the buffoonish pride with which they brandish wood-branch long arms? Men are but grown boys and will not gladly retreat just because of a little wintry weather or even snow on the ground."

He laughed softly to himself. "Why, our southern boys are just as likely to frolic and cavort in such conditions until they find themselves shot through. They are not afraid of winter; most have never truly experienced it. Only gentlemen who have traveled for business or to northward universities know what real winter weather is, and they had all creature comforts to see them through.

I thought Clark's making light of my own observations was a bit patronizing like they were silly girl inclinations. I jerked my hand from his arm and moved backward, causing his hand to fall from my cheek.

"Why, Mr. Clark Howell. You speak as if you don't believe I have any knowledge of men or the realities of such harsh existence. I may not have been in a war, but I have observed men work, sometimes under extreme conditions. I don't pretend to think it will be easy. But it's only common sense not to attempt to carry on a war in winter conditions of the north!"

Clark straightened himself and leaned forward.

"That's just it, Adeline. In war, common sense flies out the window. And anyway, we don't know that engagements will stay north. If the Union troops revamp and move southward, we may well be fighting in our Southern territories. Perhaps even right here in our beloved Georgia."

I melted towards him. "Oh darling, I don't mean to be quarrelsome. I just want us to move ahead. I want more than anything to be your wife. You know that, don't you, dearest?"

"Of course, darling, I know that. And I want nothing more than to make you that, but not at the expense of breaking your precious heart to pieces because I am away in some God-forsaken bunker freezing to death. Let us continue to make ready and prepare for that time when we will be

spouses. If we are blessed, that time will come sooner than later, but for the present, we must not rush our destiny but embrace this time of trial as an opportunity to grow that much more in love. In time, this test may refine us, as gold is purified by fire, knowing that our dedication to each other will persevere above any future misfortune."

Harriet, your father was always an eloquent speaker. At that point, I locked my eyes on his, searching for a promise.

"Oh, dear, wise, Clark. When you put it that way, I can see the sense of waiting. Yet still, I yearn for that time we can truly be as one. Please promise me we can wed as soon as reason permits. I fear if that time does not come soon, I will lose my wits completely, and then you will want nothing more than to be rid of me!"

Despite the heat of the afternoon, he crushed me to his chest. "Oh, my precious one, I will make that promise. If that time does not come soon, we may well become the couple that all others near and far will shake their heads and say, 'There goes a tarnished set! Couldn't even wait for the vows to be spoken. No wits between the two of them! Tsk tsk.'" He silenced my laughter with a full kiss on the mouth.

Oh, dear Harriet. I must pause here, before my tears ruin the ink. It's been a long letter, and I am quite overwrought recalling those early days with your father. It was a different world, before the war. I shall write again and continue the tale.

Best,

Adeline Howell

Jonesboro, Texas
March 1904

Dear Harriet,

The winter weather is moderating here in Texas. That will help the chores not be so exhausting, and hopefully, we will have a spell of pleasant spring before the oppressive heat of summer returns. I do not know how much longer I can hold out here with only Betty, Irene, and Maybell to help run things. I'm sure they will marry and leave me in a few short years. I shall have to think about leaving this farm and moving in with Park or one of my daughters if they will have me. I did truly love your father and miss him more than just his work on the farm. I miss talking with him and sharing memories. It is hard to lose the love of your life only to carry on without them. I do not think I could manage to return to Georgia as Texas truly became our home. There remains almost no family on either side still living in Georgia and no property. There are only sad memories of the war and our struggles after. I am about to get to that part of our story.

After that afternoon, when Clark and I spoke frankly about the coming war, the mood in Georgia grew even more tense. However, we still held out hope that a resolution would be found. As the summer wore on, it became painfully clear that it was not to be. The battles in Northern Virginia had intensified. By the end of August, it was clear there would be no swift resolution. As such, the local disposition among the men became one of acceptance. They would form a company of volunteers and enlist.

I was at the Howell home in Milton the day it happened. It was such a somber atmosphere. It was August 31, 1861, when Clark and his father left the house to assemble at the old meeting grounds in Warsaw. Mrs. Howell and I could no longer hold in our emotions. We had been stoic while the men told us of their intentions, but now the dam was burst. We held handkerchiefs to our weeping eyes and embraced as we waited for news.

Late afternoon, just before suppertime, Clark and his father returned. Both were reticent. Neither Mrs. Howell nor I wanted to press them for details, but of course, we could barely contain our desire to know what would happen next. We sat down to supper with only brief exchanges of minor pleasantries. The hard lines on each of our faces and the way we all avoided directly looking at each other's eyes made it obvious there was much on our minds. We each barely touched our supper. The serving girl, Pearl, removed our still-full dishes without question. I couldn't help but notice the glance exchanged between her and Mr. Howell when she brushed against him, leaning in to retrieve his plate. I'd been in the house enough by now to know that theirs was no innocent master-to-slave-girl association. I did not give it much thought, knowing that such liaisons were not uncommon, but there was more of a story behind Clark's being an only child than one might think. Oh, I'm sorry, Harriet. I am digressing into matters that are beyond my purpose in writing you these letters.

As we sat waiting for Mr. Howell's indication that the meal was over, he placed his napkin on the table and cleared his throat.

"My dear ladies, and especially you, my precious wife, Cynthia, I know you are anxious to know what the future holds. Tomorrow is the only day on which I can assuage your concerns. Clark and I are now officially enlisted in the Company of Warsaw Rebels. We will leave for Camp McDonald at Big Shanty tomorrow to begin our training. Beyond that, I cannot say. This evening may indeed be our last together as a family for some time to come. Now let us dismiss from table."

We did not speak as we retired to the parlor. The air was thick with our unspoken thoughts, but the men's silent yet palpable desire weighed most heavy in the flickering firelight. We all sat and avoided engaging in conversation or eye contact. Finally, Cynthia was the first to excuse herself, claiming the sudden developments of the day had left her head pounding. Then Hampton left the parlor to sequester himself in his study, declaring he had matters that needed his attention before the early morning departure. That left your father and I alone.

I sat in a side chair, attempting my needlework while Clark read on the divan. I pierced and pulled out the same tiny cross-stitches over and over while your father had yet to turn a single page for an entire hour. Finally, Clark closed his book.

He rose, drew the pocket doors together, then crossed the room to where I sat stabbing furiously at the fabric in my hands. I did not raise my eyes to meet his. He gently reached to pull the needlework from my hands. As the hooped cloth and thread hit the floor, the dam burst. My hands flew up to cover the heart-wrenching sobs wracking my body. He brought me into his arms, lifted me, and settled us both on the divan. We wept together.

My dear Harriet, I pray you will never know the pain of saying farewell to a sweetheart, husband, or son under the threat of war. That following morning was a nightmare. Mrs. Howell and I did not know then that our men would be in training for weeks before truly going away as soldiers. None of us, even your father or grandfather, knew much about the military. It was a relief when we received a letter within the week explaining the training process would take a few weeks. Your grandfather was elected Captain of the Company. He assured us they would be home for a visit before leaving for engagement.

Oh, my dear. It has severely drained me to recall these harrowing events. I must stop for now. I will write again soon and continue the story. I continue to long for a response from you. I suppose I cannot blame you for your lack of communication, considering our history of estrangement. Regardless, a word from my beloved eldest daughter could go far in alleviating the dreary laboriousness of my everyday existence since the passing of your father.

Best Regards,

Adeline Howell

Jonesboro, Texas

April 1904

Dear Harriet,

Spring has come to Texas, and I pray you and your family are receiving pleasant weather there in Georgia. I won't bother you with lamenting your lack of response as you clearly do not intend to respond. As I begin this letter, it is hard to imagine that the events I am about to tell you about happened so long ago, well over forty and getting close to fifty years in the past. I will try to recall what I can about the war years, but so much of that time has been lost in my conscience. Also, I prefer not to dwell on that but rather to inform you more of our life afterward about which you have expressed interest.

After their initial departure upon enlisting, it was with great relief that your grandmother Howell and I welcomed your father and grandfather home for a few days in late September. At that point, they were fully outfitted and trained for battle. She and I were not terribly concerned; the men were not yet hardened, having not seen any combat. None of us had any premonition of the horrors that would soon be visited upon them. We knew this would be our last days together before the troops left Georgia, headed north where battles were raging.

Your father and I were so in love. We knew this could be our final days on Earth together. Your Howell grandparents seemed to arrange for us to have time to ourselves quite liberally on that four-day reprieve. I shall try to put this delicately. Although it was exceedingly difficult, we managed to stay composed and chaste. After the men left and in the following months of separation, I was regretful that we had done so. All I could think was that Clark might be killed far off in Yankee territory, and I might never see him again and, as such, would have lost my "opportunity." Fortunately, that would not be the case! Mrs. Howell always retired early to her room, claiming one malady or another. On the other hand, I knew from the creaking stairs and opening and closing of doors in the late evenings that Mr. Howell took every advantage of this time with Pearl. It would be the last time any of us would see each other for months to come.

Enough of that – I shall move on with the story. We heard little the first months they were gone except that they were en route North. We would receive occasional letters, delayed by several weeks and mostly small talk, never any real news, so we never knew their precise location. Mrs. Howell and I kept up with the war through the newspaper and word of mouth. The word from the North was dire. Although the Rebels had some victories, their losses were significant. I returned to my home in Greensboro and tried to occupy my mind.

That Christmas of 1861 was the loneliest I've ever spent. The winter was harsh that year. I could only imagine the dire circumstances Clark and your grandfather must be enduring further north. We knew from reports their company had joined Wright's Brigade and moved northward to Virginia. It would take months to reach the battlefront. I knew that just a few miles north into the mountains from our Piedmont region, the weather could be severe. The few letters that came over the winter reassured us they were warmed sufficiently by campfires, stayed well-fed, and even enjoyed the occasional comforts of a welcoming home or inn, as they were still in Rebel territory.

By spring, Mrs. Howell and I both felt reassured. Our men made it through the winter and had yet to be engaged in any battle. In fact, there was one dubiously encouraging occasion. In early June, your grandfather, Captain Hampton W. Howell, sent word that he was resigning his post as of June 16 and would be returning home. The ordeals of the winter march and hardship of the circumstances convinced him war was not for a man of his age, forty-plus years old, and less than ideal fit. Clark's first cousin, Evan, son of his namesake Uncle Clark, would be named Captain.

Then, by the end of June, shortly after Mr. Howell's arrival home, the papers and unconfirmed reports showed that the company was engaging in skirmishes with the Yankees. The former captain had gotten out just in time to avoid any real danger. But our Clark was still in harm's way. Then, in July, the word of the battle at Malvern Hill near Richmond struck fear in our hearts. Over 5,000 Confederate troops were killed or wounded. I cannot express the relief we felt upon hearing from Clark that he was safe. But he also warned that the next few months were expected to be tumultuous, and I might not hear from him often. Now, I was truly beset by constant angst.

The coming months did little to relieve my worries. The word from the front after Malvern Hill was always full of numerous Confederate losses. However, they still had the upper hand in many battles and sieges. Manassas, Harper's Ferry, Antietam, and Fredericksburg followed swiftly on the heels of Malvern. After each of these, I was blessed to receive word that Clark was unscathed. Another Christmas was upon us, and I could only sit on pins and needles as the weeks wore on into 1863.

The recollection of that tense time has depleted my energy for now. The story is reaching close to the time your father and I were finally able to marry, and I want to save that telling for when I am fresh and rested. I fear I must close before I lose my wits. Again, I wish you well and refuse to give up hope of having a letter from you in return.

Regards, your mother,

Adeline Howell

in time to avoid any real danger. But our Clark was still in harm's way. Then, in July, the word of the battle at Malvern Hill near Richmond struck fear in our hearts. Over 5,000 Confederate troops were killed or wounded. I cannot express the relief we felt upon hearing from Clark that he was safe. But he also warned that the next few months were expected to be tumultuous, and I might not hear from him often. Now, I was truly beset by constant angst.

The coming months did little to relieve my worries. The word from the front after Malvern Hill was always full of numerous Confederate losses. However, they still had the upper hand in many battles and sieges. Manassas, Harper's Ferry, Antietam, and Fredericksburg followed swiftly on the heels of Malvern. After each of these, I was blessed to receive word that Clark was unscathed. Another Christmas was upon us, and I could only sit on pins and needles as the weeks wore on into 1863.

The recollection of that tense time has depleted my energy for now. The story is reaching close to the time your father and I were finally able to marry, and I want to save that telling for when I am fresh and rested. I fear I must close before I lose my wits. Again, I wish you well and refuse to give up hope of having a letter from you in return.

Regards, your mother,

Adeline Howell

San Angelo, Texas
May 1904

Dear Harriet,

The weather is already hot here in Texas. You should know that I have sold all the farm animals and utensils and moved to San Angelo to live for the time being with your sister, Eva, and her husband, William. Your sisters have assured me I will always have a home with one of them. For now, that is Eva. I have not given up hope you might write again, so the address is 228 Bird Street, San Angelo, Texas. We are at the one-year anniversary of your father's death on May 9. How I have survived this year, I do not know. Hopefully, my financial state will improve when I receive the Confederate widow's pension. William and your sister Kate's husband, Joe, have helped me with the pension application to receive your father's pension as a Confederate soldier. It has been quite a process, including getting sworn statements from Clark's cousins, Captain Evan Howell and Charles Howell, in Atlanta. Heavens, it is hard enough for me to remember all these details of the war years; how do authorities expect these aged men to recall such? Add to that the distress of grief. One's heart and mind are in no state to record details after such a loss. And that, in addition to all else that must be handled. Ah, well, let's get back to our story.

Although we had fretted heavily over the winter of 1862 into 1863, Clark's mother, father, and I were pleasantly surprised to receive word that he would be granted a furlough and should arrive back home in Georgia sometime in February. There was a lull in battles during the harshest months of December and January, and the men were badly in need of a boost of their morale.

Having experienced the fear of the previous months that I would be left alone and unmarried, I determined that Clark and I would marry during the furlough, no matter what. I boldly informed my own mother and father, who approached the Howells together. We all came to an agreement we would hurry the wedding arrangements. All of this was carried out without consulting Clark. When he arrived home, we all met him with overwhelming joy, babbling about the plans we'd made. I'm sure he immediately realized he would have no say in the matter.

We were married at the Parks Inn in Greene County on March 26, 1863. Even though the war had not yet touched Georgia soil, we did not want to appear ostentatious. We had a modest ceremony there before leaving for our new home in Milton County. His father had finished it out nicely in the months since his return, somehow knowing we would want to take immediate occupancy when Clark returned, and we could marry. The Howells, Parks, and other family from near and far came to congratulate us, even though the gathering was mostly female as so many of the men were away except for those too old or infirm to fight.

Clark was expected to return to his unit by the end of April. Fortunately, there was good news concerning his return. His transfer came through, and he would not have to return so far north. He would join the western forces. This would keep him much closer to home and hopefully out of severe weather. We knew we had only a few short weeks together. To put it tactfully, we both intended to make the most of our brief time. Oh, darling daughter, I am not so old that I don't remember those precious days and nights. I hope you and W.B. are blessed with a marriage such as your father and me. All such unions are truly desirable.

As spring passed, the battles ramped up, and the time came for your father to leave. I returned to my family in Greensboro and left Clark's parents to look after our home in Milton. As the months passed from spring to summer to fall, news of the war was dire. Chancellorsville, Gettysburg, and Manassas Gap left us stunned and more fearful, although we knew Clark was not in those vicinities. But I had my own strength. I knew I was with child, and that would carry me through. I was determined to present Clark with his child upon his return, whenever that might be. Being a mother yourself, you can understand how mixed my emotions were with excitement and trepidation. Little did I know it would be many more months and during the most turbulent time of the war before your father would arrive home to meet you.

Oh, Harriet, it pains me to remember that period when your father was so endangered. I feared not only his life but yours and mine as well. I must end here for now, as the memory causes both my heart and my bones to ache. It would improve my spirits so much to hear from you. I do hope you will consider writing soon. I'm not sure how long I will remain in San Angelo, but I will keep you apprised of my residence.

Your dearest Mother,

Adeline Howell

San Angelo, Texas
June 1904

Dear Harriet,

I hope you are well. I know your motherly and wifely duties keep you busy, but I would love to hear from you. I am counting on your heart to soften towards me and for you to seek me out as you hear more of your story. As an old woman who has been without your father for a year now, I find myself wanting to draw nearer to family. Living in San Angelo with Eva and William has been a blessing. Life is certainly easier than it was on the farm back in Jonesboro. Yet, it remains to be known if this will be a permanent arrangement.

I believe when I last left our story, I was expecting you, and your father was still away in the war. The winter beginning in 1863 was bitterly cold. I returned home to be with my family in Greene County. Considering that my father was a physician, we considered that prudent in my condition. Christmas again was lonely and barely celebrated, with so many men away in the battles. We lived as if on pins and needles and read the hospital reports voraciously, searching for names of loved ones. We did not know then that General Sherman was commencing his infamous March to the sea through Georgia. Not finding your father's name on the injured and dead list was always the brightest spot of my day. Battles had moved into North Georgia, and we all grew more anxious, not always knowing exactly where your father was.

Father put me to bed at the end of January 1864. We knew your birth was near, and he wanted to take no chances. We had arranged through trusted associates to get a message to your father as soon as possible after your birth. Finally, the day came. I remember it was a Saturday, and I prayed that you would come forth before the following Monday, an infamous Leap Day of February 29. I did not want my firstborn to have such an ominous beginning in life! Father summoned Mother and numerous servants to stand by. I do not remember much of the ordeal, as Father gave me whiskey and doses of herbs to allay my pain. Mostly, they extinguished my consciousness.

Later, knowing my need to know everything that transpired, Father described what had happened.

"Adeline, my darling, you were a brave trooper. You lay silent and unaware, your body given over to oblivious release from the pain it could no longer tolerate. But as nature dictates, it continued to work to bring the child into the world. Birthing a child, although a natural, common, and frequent function, is not for the weak in spirit or body. Your baby girl came squalling into the world, turning the cold white bedclothes to crimson red. Harriett Lucille Howell was born vigorous and healthy."

I do remember that once I regained awareness, I recoiled at the fullness of my breasts and the annoying cries of a newborn daughter. Even though I was relieved to have a healthy child, after all these years of bearing children, I can say I never took warmly to my infants those first few weeks. It is heresy for a mother to admit such. I did grow to love each child eventually, but the birthing process left me so drained it was all I could do to sustain myself. I'm sure since you've become a mother several times over, you can appreciate these sentiments. My blessed mother must have sensed my aversion. She spoke only as a mother can to a daughter.

"Adeline, darling, the child is hungry. Take her to your breast. That will help soothe her and help your own discomfort."

"Mother?" I begged in a plaintive, weakened voice. "Mother?" Is there no other way? Must I feed this child? Can't Sudie do it?"

Mother bathed my brow with a cool cloth. "No, dear. Sudie can't do it. She is indisposed. There's no telling when or even if anyone else can do it. It must be you. You're her mother."

The words fell on me like a harsh sentence. I was exhausted. Mother handed you over, and I reluctantly put you to my breast and steeled myself for the pain. As your tears ceased, mine began to flow. I could only think, why did I have to have a baby now? The war was drawing closer, Clark was still away, and we were not even settled in our new home. I wished to be anywhere but here with this writhing pain and crying child. News was that the Howell farm in Milton County was untouched, and there were still hands working on the land and the house. In Greene County, the life we'd had was no more. As soon as the ultimatum date of January 1, 1863, had come and gone without Georgia abolishing slavery or leaving the confederacy, slaves began leaving rural Greene County in droves. The Parks and Armors, unlike the wealthier Howells, did not have the means to induce them to stay. Farms were left to go fallow, and houses were consigned to be run by women who had never lifted a finger to cook, clean, or nurse a child. Now, it fell to me to nurse and care for you. Who knew how life would be, even in Milton, when this horrendous war was over. Just as milk filled my breasts with a dense heaviness, my soul filled with dread. Considering the circumstances, I did not want to be a mother at all.

This was made even worse the summer after you were born. During the battle of Atlanta, I was still with my family in Greene County, but word reached us that troops could be headed our way. Although Sherman turned south after Atlanta, it was speculated one leg of troops would continue eastward. It was decided we should depart for the Howell home in Milton County. Except for a few minor skirmishes, the war was bypassing that area. It was a good thing we made the trip back to Milton. In the fall of 1864, Greene County was overrun, and most Park properties were burned – the mill, the ferry, the bridges across the Oconee. Only the main house remained unscathed. The story goes that our Mother begged the commanding officer to spare it because her husband was a brother in Freemasons.

I know it sounds appalling that I could admit such a thing, not wanting my child. You asked how it was that you and your brother were left behind in Georgia. I am telling you the truth, as atrocious as it sounds. I am sorry your life started out under such dire conditions. Back then, fathers had little to say about the upbringing of their children, and that still holds mostly true today. I did what I had to do to provide for you.

Leaving you and Wade in Georgia when we removed to Texas seemed best at the time. This dire burden set the stage for me to steel myself against the guilt and hurt of leaving you and Wade behind. Sadly, all my life, I have not found a way around my self-reproach, until your plaintive letter of last August following your father's death. The loss of my beloved Clark and that letter put me on this sad, reflective journey of seeking mercy from the very one who was hurt the most.

I hope I have answered your question. I beg forgiveness for the pain you have experienced through trying to understand such fortuitous beginnings. I pray you can find it in your heart to accept my mother's love as it is now, full yearning for your companionship and forever desiring that we should become close before it is too late for either of us. This writing has wearied me more than any of the others. I shall have to close now.

Please respond and let me know that you hear your mother's plea with favor so that I may hear from you and relieve my soul of this burden. I may not write again as my bones are weary, my mind wanders, and my constitution is weak. It pains me so to think I caused you so much heartache.

With unbounding love and affection, your Mother,

Adeline Howell

HARRIET RESPONDS

Gainesville, Georgia
June 1910

Dear Mother,

I pulled out your last few letters and read them again. I realize now it has been six years since I last heard from you. I can't say I received those letters you wrote in the year after Father's death in the spirit in which you hoped. That is partly why I have not written back until now. I can't say I have totally forgiven that my brother and I were given away to our grandparents. I have been a mother myself many times over now, with five daughters and five sons, losing one of our precious boys soon after birth. I still cannot fathom giving away any of my children at any age, even knowing they would be cared for.

An event has occurred that has helped me understand the heartache you have born since Father died. My darling, my husband, William, has passed on. He was suddenly ill on the first of May this year. It was discovered he harbored an infection from an abscessed tooth. The infection went into his blood, and the poisoning was so intense he could not be saved, and death took him on May 8th. The children and I have been in quite a state of shock. Howell, Charlie, Bessie, Maude, Tommie, and Ernest are all still at home. The others have married and moved on to start their own families. I do not yet know how we will manage. We shall all have to do what we can for income and try to live on it. I loved my William dearly, and as a family, we always had a grand time. He was a good father and a good provider and will be sorely missed.

So, dear Mother, I shall try to write occasionally. I still have the younger children to take care of, but in a few years, I shall be able to travel to Texas to reunite with you and my other family members. Having lost so many dear ones, I do long for family ties. However, I will not travel until I feel my youngest are able to manage on their own. I hope your health will continue to hold until the time we may be together again.

Sincerely, your daughter,

Harriet Howell Smith

MY REFLECTION ONE

Finally, Harriet responded, but it was six years later. I was dumbfounded. Reading the letters was a voice drifting down through decades. The barbecue Adeline described was like a scene straight out of Gone with the Wind! I'd always heard we had ancestors who enslaved people, were wealthy landowners, and fought in the Civil War. That's not so uncommon among those of us in the South. But to have it confirmed in writing was another thing.

Now, what was I to do with such information? Should I feel guilty about the status of my ancestors as enslavers? I can't even entertain the thought of not being repulsed by the revelation. Should I be proud? I could not, but I have heard some boast about ancestors enslaving people and owning huge plantations. Adeline seemed to allude that their feelings about slavery were ambiguous. Yes, it was a different time, but does that absolve one of responsibility? It was inspiring to read the frankness with which Adeline described her feelings. Her father and her husband, Clark, sounded like wise men. Were they typical of men at that time?

It is hard to imagine the wealth that was there in those pre-Civil War years. This great-great-grandmother and great-grandmother were obviously well off, in contrast to my mother and grandmother, who were poor, working-class folk. I knew little about my great-grandmother, the silent Harriet, recipient of Adeline's letters. It was clear from Adeline's letters that Harriet harbored bitterness toward her mother.

That is not an entirely unfamiliar feeling, as you will learn later. I suppose it shouldn't be surprising under the circumstances, but there had to be more to the story. Adeline did sound remorseful, especially in that last letter. Did she and Harriet ever resolve their differences? Why did Harriet wait six years to respond? Did they ever reunite? Was the wealth never to be recovered?

The way Adeline and Cynthia stoically faced their men going off to war was something else I could not fathom. My own mother had seen my father off during WWII and my brother off to Vietnam. I knew at least one grandfather had served in the military, but not in an actual war. I did not have personal experience with this heart-wrenching experience. However, I would have plenty of others of my own.

Then suddenly, to hear from Harriet. Why did she wait six years to respond to her mother? She must have known her mother was still alive. To read the sudden announcement of my great-grandfather's death, William, was eerily reminiscent of Adeline's sudden announcement of her beloved Clark's death just a few years before in Texas. Now Harriet is in the same position, a widow with children, albeit younger children than those Adeline had been left with.

There were more packets tied in ribbons in the letter box. Would they reveal more of Harriet and Adeline's lives? Would more voices from the past answer the many questions I had? When I returned to the letter box and the next packet of letters, it was clear from the postmark that there would be even more time and distance between the first set of letters and the next.

The first letter in the next packet had a postmark of December 1923, Hapeville, Georgia. Scribbled in pencil across the front were the words

"Tommie and Harriet." It was addressed to Harriet Shankle in Waco, Texas. What? Is Harriet Smith now Harriet Shankle? This was confusing. Tommie was my grandmother, and my mother had just been born in November of 1923. Why had so many years elapsed between letters? As I read on, it became clear there was a rhyme and reason. Just as Harriet had written to her own mother expressing her bitterness at being left behind, her daughter, Tommie, would express feelings of the same kind. Harriet, in turn, would attempt to assuage her daughter's feelings just as her own mother had done for her.

PART TWO

HARRIET, MY GREAT-GRANDMOTHER, AND TOMMIE BELLE

TOMMIE BELLE TO HER MOTHER HARRIET

Hapeville, Georgia
December 1923

Dear Mother,

I hope this letter and Christmas greetings find their way to you. I am sending it to the last address I have for you in Waco. Since I haven't heard from you, I am not sure if you are still at that location. I know you missed Mr. Shankles after his untimely death, but I did hope you would spend some time with us before setting out for Texas. There are several items of news I have for you.

Clarence and I are now in Hapeville, just outside Atlanta. He is working in the shirt factory. Most importantly, you should know that you are now the grandmother of two more little girls! Of course, you knew we had Adeline Christine, she being born in February of 1919 before you left for Texas. I had hoped for your return or at least to hear from you so I could tell you we had Bessie Lucille in May 1921. Just a few weeks ago, on November 17, 1923, we had Mary Elizabeth. Three little girls! I am happy with them, and Clarence is too. He doesn't seem disappointed not to have a little boy.

We left Commerce when baby Lucille was barely a year old. Times were hard and work in the overall factory was hard on Clarence. The work here in the shirt factory is hard, too. We see Earle and Bessie often since they are close by, but the others are too far away or too busy with their own lives. So here I am, a young married mother with three little babies and no real family close by. I know you had a passel of young'uns to take care of, too, but usually, there was family to help. I would be most relieved if you came back to Georgia and lived near us. I fear my girls won't know their grandmother, and with Father gone over eleven years now, the memories fade, and I may not even have recalled telling them stories of him. I am sure there are going to be times in the future when I will need advice on raising young ladies, and there will be no one to turn to. We are barely scraping by now, and life is hard enough as it is. I know the extra affection of a grandmother, which I myself did not have, could mean so much to the girls as they grow older. How I would love them to hear your piano playing if we only had a piano!

I do hope you are well. Please tell me if there is news from family out there – have you been able to rekindle ties with your brother or sisters? How is your mother? I understand now how much you must have missed her all these years, as I do you. What I don't understand is how the mothers in our family can leave their daughters. Of course, with me being the last of five girls, maybe you'd had your fill, and your own mother did not set a very good pattern for you to follow. Sometimes, I whisper promises to my babies that I will never desert them.

Well, Mother, I don't mean to complain so, I am just feeling low and maybe a bit abandoned. I keep busy with the girls and take on odd jobs like sewing or laundry. You know Clarence can be demanding, and I try to be a good wife, but I do not want any more babies any time soon. I must go now; the baby is hungry. We may move around some, too, hoping to find enough work to support ourselves, but I will try to keep you apprised of our address. I hope to hear from you soon. More than anything, I would love to see you back here with us.

Your loving youngest daughter,

Tommie Belle

HARRIET RESPONDS TO TOMMIE

Waco, Texas
January 1924

Dear Tommie,

I am so glad your letter found its way to me. I'm happy to hear you and Clarence and the babies are well. I do hope you all had a good Christmas despite your hardships. I have moved around, staying with various relatives, but more about that later.

First, I want to address some of the concerns you wrote about in your letter to me. Your letter reminded me of one I wrote to my own mother back in 1903. It expressed many similar thoughts. In response, she wrote a series of letters over a year's time that explained much about her actions. I can't say I accepted those letters in the frame of mind she wished. In fact, I did not even respond for several years, until 1910 to be exact, after the death of your father. I intend to write similarly to you, hoping it will help you understand my actions. It's beginning to seem like the women in our family have all had troubles to bear.

You spoke of feelings of abandonment. I am so sorry about that. Believe me, I know well what that can be like. I suppose, once you were married and Ernest went off to join the Navy, I felt unneeded and a bit relieved. I'd longed for years to come to Texas, hoping to rekindle a relationship with my own mother and get to know my sisters. I saw my opportunity after the death of Mr. Shankles. Twice widowed, no husband, no children at home. Nothing to keep me from leaving Georgia. But let me back up a few years and tell you more leading up to this.

Oh, Tommie, just imagine how I felt as a young child, knowing my own mother and father had given me away to my grandparents. Yes, they tried to explain it away with all the advantages that arrangement offered, but those things mean little to a child who wants nothing more than the love of her own Mother and Father. Then, it was inexplicable when they did the same with my baby brother Wade. Every two to three years, another baby would come along for Mother and Father. Yet, we were the only two to remain with our grandparents. Your grandfather and great-grandfather's home were on adjoining property, so it wasn't like we never saw them. Still, at the end of the day, Wade and I went home to Grandpapa and Grandmama. I did enjoy the advantages we had there – good food, lovely surroundings, pets, and farm animals. The household servants, most of them former slaves who had stayed on to work for next to nothing wages and their own living accommodations, doted on me, too. I spent hours in Mary's kitchen listening to stories from the old days and learning songs with no name. One of my favorite pastimes as a child was playing on their piano. All homes of a certain social class were expected to have a piano, and young ladies were required to learn to play. I took to it naturally and taught myself to play by ear, mastering many tunes. I was doing so well on my own that formal lessons did not seem necessary, so that's how I continued.

By the time I was eight years old, I was in school at the small local Warsaw school. My Uncle Singleton, Cousin Evan, and sometimes even my father, Clark, served as teachers at the school. The surrounding farms had many children between the Howells, the Grahams, the Jacksons, and others. I led a sheltered life on Grandfather's farm, but I adored school and relished having friends and the adoration of the teachers. I don't know if the teachers felt pity for me knowing my family situation. My grandparents and parents were not rich exactly, but certainly not poor. I didn't know at the time how precarious their finances were. Children are not aware of such things until they become pronounced. The Civil War left many landowners in dire straits. Your father and grandfather were among those who tried to maintain a fine standard of living, or at least the appearance of one, to no avail.

We managed all right, but then my life changed substantially. Grandpapa sold his property in Milton County and moved across the river to Duluth, where several relatives were still living. He was appointed postmaster at Duluth, and he and Grandmama lived a frugal life there. During the time I attended school and lived with my grandparents, my father and Grandfather began making frequent trips to Texas, hoping to find property and settle there.

For a while, my mother and father still resided in Milton and grew their family. I had three brothers and two sisters. Two of the brothers were twins, but sadly, only one survived infancy. Still, Mother and Father had a full house. They brought Wade back to live with them, as an extra farm hand. It was getting harder and harder to support the family with farming, so Father finally made the move to Texas, and Mother would follow.

By the time I turned sixteen, there were few opportunities for girls to continue their education. I had no idea what might become of me, but fate would intervene. Just the year before, in 1879, the new Georgia Baptist Female Seminary was founded in Gainesville, what you know now as Brenau Academy. It was considered a prestigious but affordable academy for young ladies. The fees were nominal, and it offered music training, for which I had shown proclivity. Our strangely arranged family was separated further. I went west to board at the school in Gainesville. Grandpapa and Grandmama were east in Duluth, Mother was in Milton with the younger children, and Father was in Texas. At sixteen, I had no idea where my life was heading. I simply gave it no thought, occupying my day-to-day existence with whatever activities were at hand. After all, I'd been abandoned once and was accustomed to moving about.

Oh dear, the time has flown as I've recalled my early years. I know those circumstances do not excuse any choices I've made, although I do hope you will have an understanding heart. Life is so very different now. I will save the continued story for another time. I think you will find encouragement as I proceed to describe love, life, marriage, and having young children in quick succession. Tommie, so many women struggle in silence during such challenging times and end up paying the price later.

I do hope you, Clarence, and the baby girls are all well and can find joy in your present situation. Please write and send me a photograph if you have any. I will try to keep you apprised of my address.

Sincerely,

Your Loving Mother
HHS

Waco, Texas
February 1924

Dear Tommie,

I hope this letter finds you, Clarence, and the children well. Winter can be a trying time with coughs and running noses. I am sure you are busy trying to stay warm, fed, and keeping the ill spirits away. I hope and pray that Clarence has found work, and that you are at least not starving. I haven't had a response to my last letter, so have to assume you all are managing all right.

I've seen my mother some, but she is over in San Angelo with my sister Alma. At eighty years old, she is still going strong. We are cordial with each other but do not have the close relationship I longed for. I want to resume telling you about my life at an important time of change when I was sixteen.

In the fall of 1880, I entered the recently established Georgia Baptist Female Seminary. My life was turned upside down. I lived there in a dormitory with other girls from across the Southeast, a completely different way of life from that to which I was accustomed.

I'll tell you a little bit about life in boarding school. I've always felt sorry that you never had this experience like your older sisters. By the time you were of that age, the finances simply were not available. I'm not sure how my own family managed it for me, as their own plight was growing more serious, but more about all that later.

From being the adored granddaughter in a well-appointed home to being just one of a group of girls in adequate yet spartan living accommodations was quite an adjustment for me. About twenty of us each had a bed and bureau in a large room upstairs in the big house. We shared bath facilities down the hall. We all ate together at specific times in the downstairs dining room. The food was acceptable but not so delicious as what Mary prepared at home. We were responsible for all the cleaning and taking care of our personal belongings and laundry. All of this had to be accomplished around a full schedule of classes, limited free time, and a strict timetable of being inside the house and lights out.

I enjoyed getting to know other girls from various regions and circumstances. The Academy was set up to enable girls of differing classes to afford an education. Having lived a sheltered and rural life, I relished hearing about cities, townhomes, automobiles, gay social events, and even a few romantic dalliances. I knew nothing about any of that and certainly had no experience with any of it.

My classes included arithmetic, grammar, composition, history, literature, and French. I excelled in all except for French. Foreign language was exactly that for me, foreign! Interspersed with all of these were bookkeeping and penmanship. In addition, due to my natural talent at the piano, I was enrolled in music classes. Although the more formal and technical aspects of music had never been a part of my repertoire, I suppose the knowledge did enhance my playing. As it turned out, as you already know, it would be an advantage for me later in life.

Not to say that it was all study and drudgery. We played games and engaged in mischievous antics. Of course, we were always well supervised. No men were ever allowed at our living quarters. On rare occasions, we were invited out to social or cultural events in town where we could meet young men. My, but those were thrilling! It would be one of those events that would change my life forever.

I know I never talked much about these experiences with you, but I feel it's important you hear about them now so that you will know your mother was once more than an old, tired-out woman with a passel of children. With your older sisters Adeline, Bessie, and Daisy, school was discussed as the time approached for each of them to attend. By the time you and Maude were approaching that age, your father had passed, and formal education was not an option I could entertain for you two youngest girls. It broke my heart, but there's more to that story I will reserve for later.

The important thing I want you to know is that I did not start out to become a vagabond, absent mother, or grandmother. Then again, most people don't end up as what they set out to become. Our choices and fate tend to intervene in the dreams of the young and hopeful. My dear, I am growing tired and quite melancholy recalling those long-ago days for you, and I don't mean to dash your sentiment, so I will stop for now.

Please write and let me know how you all are.

Always,

Your loving mother
HHS

Waco, Texas
March 1924

Dear Daughter,

I am disappointed not to have heard from you, although I do realize you are busy with those girls. Let me think, will Christine be five this year, and Lucille will be three? And, of course, the baby, Mary, will be one in November. I know you have your hands full with three little ones. I imagine Clarence is a handful, too. He'll be wanting to try for a boy soon. Do what you can to avoid having another baby so soon. I know from experience that you will wear yourself out, especially with the money troubles. Hopefully, Clarence has found some steady work. Well, enough about that.

I've been scraping by teaching piano lessons and doing a few odd jobs here and there. I hope you don't mind me telling you that I have a couple of gentlemen friends, too. They are fine men, though not rich! They are good for company and conversation and an occasional supper out for entertainment. I am not looking to get married again. Having a taste of independent living has been refreshing, and times are changing. I have not made any headway with my sisters, brother, or mother. We write occasionally, but I do not see them often. They are mostly in the San Angelo area except for Estelle, who is in California, like your brother Charlie. I don't know what the attraction out there is – no gold rush nowadays like that which benefitted the Summerours after the small rush in Georgia played out.

Let me get back to my story. During my two years at the seminary, I was close enough to home to visit frequently. But it was the social events in town I really liked. It was one of those in December of 1881 that would change my life. Just before school was dismissed for Christmas, a soirée was held at the magnificent new Piedmont Hotel. All the ladies from the seminary were invited, as were many young unmarried gentlemen of good upbringing from Gainesville and surrounding towns. It was there that I met your father.

The weather was mild that December. We young ladies were glad about that because it meant we wouldn't need wraps to wear to the big party, covering our festive gowns. You should have heard us as we dressed in the dormitory.

"Oh, Lucy, that gown is gorgeous. The yellow sets off your auburn hair."

"My, my, Amanda, if Jackson doesn't notice you in that stunning green silk, he must be blind."

"Dear Constance, let me pin up that stray curl in the back. Some chaperone will think you've had a man's fingers caress your hair!"

We all laughed at that one especially. We were kept sheltered but had our private speculations. Some of the girls were more experienced than others, so matters of men and romance were common knowledge. We'd all seen babies born at home. I felt a bit saucy in my own royal blue taffeta, blue eyes, and shining coal-black hair. We finished tying on the bustle frames, arranging our hair up, stepping into gowns, and pulling our decolletage as low as we thought would pass inspection. Even if it were pulled up by one of the school marms, we could smooth it back down. Gathering our reticule, gloves, and hats, we set out for the grand event.

I kept close to my best friend, Julia. We rode in one of the many carriages that had been requisitioned from some of the town's wealthier families. The town saw the whole event to show off its elegant new hotel, the Academy's promising young women, and even its most desirous eligible bachelors. All the local businesses and townspeople were standing by to witness the spectacle as we arrived at the Piedmont. A line of white waist-coated servants stood ready to hand us down. More significant was the crowd of young men who stood about watching as we young ladies were paraded to the entrance. It was so hard to avert our eyes, trying not to stare! Some of the girls had managed to acquire suitors and were expecting to pair off once we were inside. I was not one of those girls, but I hoped to be by the end of the evening. I would be eighteen in a couple of months, an old maid! And I knew the money for school was waning. I felt like I needed to find a prospective husband, and the sooner, the better.

Once inside, the unattached ladies stood aside or gathered around the refreshments. I was gazing at the dancing couples and keeping an eye on Julia and her beau, who edged closer to the open veranda doors. I did not see the man who approached me from the side until he cleared his throat loudly and spoke.

"Good evening, Miss Howell. May I introduce myself?"

I turned and found myself speechless.

Oh dear, there's my next student, I hear them at the door. I did not intend to get so carried away with the details. Once my memories begin to unfold like roses in spring, it's hard to make them stop. Sorry to leave you anticipating what's next, but you are wise enough to know what happens. I will write again soon, providing the details.

Take care, dear Tommie. I remain as ever,

Your loving mother.
HHS

Waco, Texas
April 1924

Dear Daughter,

Hello Tommie. I hope this letter finds you and the children well. I imagine little Mary is getting bigger these days, and the other girls are enjoying getting out in the spring weather. Spring has arrived here in Texas, but I do recall how beautiful this time of year was in Georgia. It also signaled the time when work was compounded as the men pushed to get the crops in. With you in the city now, I doubt that is much of a factor. I do hope Clarence has found work that will at least keep you and the children fed and clothed.

I continue to get by teaching my piano lessons. I visit occasionally with family but have failed to feel a true part of their lives. I suppose the damage done by our separation early in life is irreparable. Although it's easy to say that is all in the past now, not to dwell on it, there is a part of my life on which I love to reminisce. I believe I was cut short the last time I wrote, but I have allowed plenty of time to tell it to you now. It is about how I met and fell in love with your father.

I did not really know your father before that evening at the lovely dance at the Piedmont Hotel just before Christmas in 1881, but I did know of him. I had seen him about town from time to time. He was considered one of the most eligible and sought-after bachelors thereabouts. He worked in his father's business – a general store and livery that was well-established in town. You know some of the plain facts about your father but did not really get to know him as a man due to his untimely death when you were barely eleven.

I was surprised when W.B. approached me that evening. He was considered one of the most eligible men in town, as the oldest son of the former mayor and a well-respected businessman. There appeared to be little more than that to make him attractive to any young ladies from the academy. He had no reputation as a ladies' man. Indeed, he was thought to be quiet, reserved, and more involved in his work than socializing. His appearance was plain and soft. Oh yes, we ladies had profiled most of the eligible men around town. He was not high on the list as a dashing suitor but was a respectable prospect. As it became clear he was making his way towards me, I was prepared to be cordial and mildly interested.

"Good evening, Miss Howell. May I introduce myself?"

"Of course you may, but it seems you already know my name, Mr. Smith."

A sheepish grin and slight blush accompanied his stammer.

"Um, well, you would be correct. And you know my name as well. My sister Kate is in first year at the academy, and she has mentioned you. Also, I believe my father has done business with some of your relations."

"Ah, I see. And you are not completely unknown to me, Mr. Smith. The ladies of the academy are aware of the eligible men in town."

The shy smile and blush bloomed again.

"Um, er, uh. Is that so? Hmm."

There proceeded a few seconds of awkward silence. Then, "Miss Howell, if I may be presumptuous, would you care to dance?"

It was my turn to present a slight smile, which I did happily, but I did not bid the color that came forth on my own cheek.

Mr. Smith and I danced, then returned to my waiting place near the wall where there were empty chairs now that the ice had been broken and more couples had taken to the dance floor. He did not seem inclined to take his leave of me but offered to gather refreshments for the two of us. We had easy conversations, mostly about our fathers and families. He was soft but well-spoken, with nothing but kindness to relay about his family and mine. I got the distinct feeling he knew much more about my family than he'd first let on. We danced more and engaged in further conversation. As the evening concluded, we only spoke and danced with each other.

The chaperones began to gather us young ladies to head out to the waiting carriages. I'm sure it was a presumptive effort to eliminate the possibility of anything more than a chaste good evening by our suitors. Mr. Smith escorted me out and gave my hand to a servant to help me up into an elegant carriage.

"Simon, you take care to get Miss Smith and these other young ladies back to the seminary safely. Return my carriage here, and I'll take it home."

"Yes, sir, Mr. Smith. I'll do exactly that." A broad smile streaked the servant's face, and I thought I caught a wink of his eye.

"Good night, Miss Howell. I wish you a happy Christmas and hope to see you again soon."

I was so taken aback by this exchange I stumbled over my words.

"Um, yes, Mr. Uh, Smith. Thank you for a pleasant evening." As the carriage began to move, I turned back and saw Mr. Smith still standing in place right where he had been since he gave my hand to Simon. I called out,

"Oh! And Mr. Smith, a happy Christmas to you as well."
My heart opened a tiny bit as I raised my hand in farewell.

Oh my, those memories seem like a lifetime ago, and indeed they were. I suppose that's enough of the story for now. The telling of it has put me in quite a state of melancholy. I shall go and find something else to occupy my mind. Write soon and send photographs of the girls if you can manage. I'd love to see them.

Your loving mother,
HHS

Waco, Texas
May 1924

Dear Daughter,

First, I want to say I'm sorry if the close of my last letter was less than positive. I know the etiquette of writing back and forth, always ending with an encouraging word, but I just couldn't find it in me at the time. Now, I will break another rule of politeness. I must say I am disappointed I haven't heard from you. I know you are overwhelmed with three babies and a useless husband. Or is it that you are still angry with me for leaving Georgia? I can't necessarily blame you. I am a master at feelings of abandonment. I suppose it runs in the family even though I was still just a child, really, unmarried anyway, when my mother and father left me behind in Georgia to pursue happiness in Texas. What a surprise they got. More heat, dirt, and hard work. Well, that's their story, not mine.

Sorry, I know this sounds petty and cranky. I'm just very tired. The spring recital schedule is demanding. And the parents are all such nervous wrecks over their little darlings' performances, I spend as much time reassuring them as I do the children. Unfortunately, there are no budding concert pianists this season. No young Vladimir Horowitz in the whole bunch. It will be over in a week or so, and I'll start the visiting circuit. Mother is still living with Alma and Joe in San Angelo, so I suppose I'll start there.

Now, let me think. Where did I leave off last time? I think it was right after I first met your father. The Christmas after that dance was meager and boring. Mother was expecting Estelle at that time and had four other children at home. Father was preoccupied with worry and grandiose plans of moving to Texas. Grandmother and Grandfather seemed tired. I tried to be cheerful for the younger children, but fear I was not successful. All I could think about was getting back to Gainesville and hopefully seeing your father again soon. I wasn't quite sure yet how I was going to arrange it, but it was always in the forefront of my mind.

When school resumed in January, it was unusually warm. I made my plan. I knew W.B. worked in his father's store. I had managed to save a few dollars back from Christmas and invented a story that I needed supplies for the new classes. Young ladies were allowed to walk into town during the daytime if we were in groups of three or more. Seriously, did the house mothers think we girls wouldn't conspire among ourselves to have unsupervised time alone with someone? Of course, I was still weeks away from that circumstance, but the first time bode well for future encounters.

"Good afternoon, ladies. May I be of assistance? I surmise such young ladies as you are not here for purchasing housewares."

I don't think Mr. Smith recognized me at first. I decided to let one of the others take the lead. Julia stepped back as Connie spoke up. "Why yes, Mr. Smith. Could you show us what you have in the way of stationery?"

The group moved towards the side of the store. I followed along but then stepped into a side aisle where there were pens and ink. After giving the group near the stationery time to get involved in conversation, I emerged and interrupted Mr. Smith.

"Mr. Smith? I have some questions about pens and ink. Could you look at them with me?"

W.B. looked taken aback at first, but then the recognition brought a light to his eyes.

"But, of course, Miss Howell. Ladies, please excuse me. I'll be just over here if you need anything." He turned to me and took my elbow, but not before Connie, Julia, and I could exchange glances and triumphant smiles.

When it was just the two of us in the other aisle, I picked up a bottle of ink and turned to face him. As I did so, his hand closed over the ink, his fingertips brushing mine.

"This is an excellent choice, Miss Howell."

"Really, Mr. Smith? And what makes it so?"

"The quality. It's the best we have. That does, however, make it the most expensive."

I jerked my hand away, replaced the bottle on the shelf, and cleared my throat.

"Well then. That's that." I turned a bright smile on Mr. Smith.

"Oh no. Here, take it." Mr. Smith placed the little bottle in my hand. "You know, I've been hoping to run into you. May I call on you at the seminary? I'd like to see you again."

I smiled shyly. "I understand my grandfather has a standing account here. Please charge the ink to him."

Mr. Smith's solemn face broke into a broad smile. "That I will do, Miss Howell. Thank you for your business."

A titter came from the end of the aisle as Connie and Julia quickly averted their eyes and covered their mouths.

"You are welcome, Mr. Smith. I'll just take this in my bag. I look forward to seeing you soon."

The three of us smiled demurely and sashayed out of the store. No stationery was purchased.

So that is how my second encounter with your father went. After that, things moved swiftly.

Oh my, look at the time. My darling Tommie, my baby girl, I must go and prepare for this evening's recital. Recalling those precious first days

W.B. and I had together makes me miss you and the others that much more. I've never really told you how much I regretted that you and Ernest did not get the same advantages as your older sisters and brothers. I am terribly sorry for that, but it's a story for another time.

I'm not sure if I will be at any one address over the summer, but if you write send something to Alma's address and it will catch up to me eventually. Kiss the babies for me, Tommie. It would be so wonderful to at least see a photo of them. I have no idea what they look like!
I love you all.

Your loving Mother,

HHS

San Angelo, Texas
June 1924

Dear Tommie,

How are you? I'm sure summer has arrived in Georgia as it has in Texas. It is hot as blue blazes here. Fortunately, Alma, Mother, and I do not have to overly exert ourselves except for some regular household chores. Alma has help some days. We can't expect Mother to carry much of the load at almost eighty-one. Alma is fifty-four, and I'm sixty now. Alma's husband Joe is almost seventy, but he still does work some. He's considered one of the best bootmakers in San Angelo. They manage well financially and own their home. With no children, they are best suited to having Mother live with them and for me to visit for extended periods, but I still try not to wear out my welcome. Of course, I am closest to Alma of all my sisters, with her being the next in age other than my brother Wade. I haven't corresponded with Wade in years since he settled in Alabama. Mother has also lived with my youngest sister, Irene, at times. She's also here in San Angelo.

Mother still has most of her senses. We talk some, but mostly about trivialities and day-to-day happenings. I can't get her to talk much about the past. It was twenty years ago she wrote to me that series of letters telling me about her and Father, the war years, and the days when I was young. It is as if she got it all out then and closed off that part of her life like an attic door, leaving the past to molder away. She continues to hold it against me that I had so much resentment toward her and Father for leaving me in Georgia. Alas, that is done and over, and I wouldn't have you, my darling baby girl Tommie, or your siblings had I not remained back East.

Enough of that. I will resume the story of my and your father's romance. In those days, men were allowed to call on us young ladies at the seminary during certain hours and conditions. Your father began to make regular visits each Sunday, and we would occasionally go on outings with groups of others. Just as at the store, we girls could usually connive to steal a few private minutes alone with our beaus. Indeed, it was left to my ingenuity to make such moments happen. Although your father was a dear man, and I came to love him immensely, he was not bold when it came to romance. I was the first to take his hand and to lean in for that first kiss.

Although an independent young man, your father was still living at his own father's home when we first started seeing each other. I was invited to their home often and got to know his family well. He had an older half-brother and three older half-sisters from his father's first marriage. His mother, Permelia, was twenty-four years younger than his father. Your father was her oldest child, born in 1860, with six younger siblings to follow. She was still bearing children over twenty years later. When we began seeing each other at the first of 1882, your grandmother Permelia was expecting. She would go on to give birth twice more, both as I was expecting. That woman was a saint. It's amazing she is still living today at eighty-four. Like my own mother, women of that time endured hard lives and kept going. Their hard lives and sometimes hard hearts enabled them to survive.

Back to your father and me. Your father purchased his own home with a loan from his father in the late spring of 1882. I finished my second and final year at the Seminary that May. I took a room lodging in town and worked teaching music lessons. Although we were discreet, it became much easier for your father and I to spend time alone with each other. He sought my advisement furnishing his home. It seemed all but assumed it would be our home. As things went, W.B. became more at ease away from his overbearing father's presence and the jumble of life at his home. It was like he'd been released from familial duties to finally become his own person.

Now, Tommie, you are a woman grown and married, and it should not disconcert you for me to speak of such things. Let's just say your father was no longer so reticent when it came to amour. We often stopped walking near my place of lodging, where trees shaded the sidewalk in the evening and stole kisses in the dark. It was during one of those heated moments of desire that it happened. Your father broke from our embrace and held me at arm's length, whispering with heavy breath.

"My darling Harriet. I know I don't have much in goods, an entertaining personality, a handsome appearance, or alluring charms, but I do have a sincere heart and all my love to offer you. I cannot wait any longer to have you myself. Please tell me you will agree to be my wife, the mistress of my home, and the mother of my children."

I can hear those words in my heart as if it were only yesterday. My response? Yes! Yes! And yes! We were officially engaged and set a wedding date for September.

My darling Tommie, I must go for now. Give my love to your babies. Will write again in a few weeks.

Best, your mother,

HHS

at arm's length, whispering with heavy breath.

"My darling Harriet. I know I don't have much in goods, an entertaining personality, a handsome appearance, or alluring charms, but I do have a sincere heart and all my love to offer you. I cannot wait any longer to have you myself. Please tell me you will agree to be my wife, the mistress of my home, and the mother of my children."

I can hear those words in my heart as if it were only yesterday. My response? Yes! Yes! And yes! We were officially engaged and set a wedding date for September.

My darling Tommie, I must go for now. Give my love to your babies. Will write again in a few weeks.

Best, your mother,

HHS

San Angelo Texas
July 1924

Dear Tommie,

I hope this letter finds you and the children well, and Clarence also. I know working in a factory is arduous at this time of year and can take a toll on one's disposition. Hopefully, the children can find some respite from the heat and can stay cool. I am glad that Clarence has gainful employment in the city. Baby Mary must be about to creep around. She and the other two girls must keep you busy. Cleaning, cooking, laundry, and seeing to Clarence's needs must leave you exhausted.

No real news from here in Texas. As usual, it is hot here. San Angelo is a bustling town – cattle are coming through, and the oil boomers are raucous and noisy. Money seems to flow freely. Mother is maintaining her own, although she is a bit feeble. Not in her wits, mind you, but in body. She doesn't talk much, especially about the old days. She never speaks of Maybell, the sister I lost in 1920, having never actually known her as an adult. She did marry but had no children. I try to draw Mother out in hopes of learning more, but alas, I am dependent upon the letters she wrote years ago. Hopefully, I will return to Georgia eventually, and you and I will have time to share more of our lives with each other.

I believe I left off last time just as your father and I were about to be married. Looking back, I find it interesting that both my own mother and your father's mother had babies born near the time of our marriage. My baby sister Estelle was born in April before we married, and W.B.'s sister Alma was born in July. We were also pleased that by marrying in September, my father would be in Georgia, rather than gallivanting around Texas.

Your father had come out of his shell more after leaving his father's house, but he was still not a jovial man. He was reserved and just as happy to remain sitting aside others enjoying his solitude as to partaking in frivolity. He was kind and loving in his own way, though not dashing or demonstrative with his affections. Let me speak frankly, woman to woman. I was the only one who knew of his amorous nature in the confines of our own bedroom. None would have suspected his prowess from his outward behavior.

After the wedding in Duluth at my grandfather's church, we made our home in the house on Broad Street in Gainesville. I saw my mother, sisters, and brother now and then over in Warsaw. I was secretly relieved not to be expected to help my mother with her now six children (and two more to come.) My father was away in Texas most of the time. I find it poignant that this is the case now, with my being here and you there in Georgia so close to the same period of your life. During that first year of our marriage, your father took a position in the Hall County court. He was able to gradually shed his responsibilities to his father's business and become even more independent. Almost nine months to the day after our wedding, your oldest sister, Adeline Christine, was born in May of 1883.

The circle was about to commence again as it often did in those days. Women married young, and babies came along every couple of years. It happened with my own grandmother, my mother, and myself. I am pleased that this cycle is weakening for my own children. Of course, I love each and every one of you, but a lifetime of childbearing takes a toll on a woman, especially when times are hard. My daughters are embracing a less demanding life, and I hope that is the case for you.

I am sorry if I sound like all doom and gloom, for that was not the case whilst living in those days. Ours was a content home full of laughter and music. Yes, we worked hard. W.B. was often away at the court. Running a household and taking care of what would eventually be ten children was demanding. With you being the baby girl and Ernest the youngest of all, you wouldn't remember those days. I do hope your older siblings recall those days with fondness.

Oh dear, here I go, rambling again. I would love to hear from you. I hear Atlanta is a city teeming with industry and business. The papers here report there is no lack of availability of spirits or crime associated with producing them. The women's temperance groups are quite active here in San Angelo, although personally, I find the whole debacle of little importance. There are much worse crimes that should be under investigation. There I go, rambling again.

In any event, please write and send pictures of the girls. I am sure they are little darlings. Take care of them and yourself. I do hope you find some joy in your little family despite working so hard. I shall write again next month.

Your loving mother,

HHS

San Angelo, Texas
August 1924

Dearest daughter,

I pray this letter finds you well. I must assume you are busy with your life since I have yet to hear from you since I began writing back in January. I will be leaving San Angelo in a few weeks, for Waco. My welcome is wearing thin, and I have made no progress in establishing close relationships with my family here, as much as I wanted to.

I do want to tell you more of my story in hopes of gaining your understanding. I know you desire for me to return to Georgia, and that may yet happen at some point in the future, but I cannot say when. It all depends on what opportunities life offers.

As I said in the last letter, during my years married to your father was agreeable. Your older brothers and sisters continued to arrive every couple of years. I also had two additional sisters born; your father had another sister and brother. You can rest assured that you won't be put in the position of being an expecting mother at the same time as your own mother!

You were my baby girl, and Ernest, my baby boy, but only because of my darling baby Park. Born in September 1904, he only lived until Christmas. Sickly from birth, we all grieved his death. There is nothing worse than for a mother to lose a child. My Mother lost an infant twin brother to my own brother Park, for whom we named our lost baby. She has also lost an adult daughter. I pray my children will all survive me and none of you experience the horrendous loss of any of my grandchildren.

Your father worked hard all those years when we raised children, but education was still expensive. He borrowed money against his inheritance from his father, old W.P., who lived to the age of 75. That provoked dire circumstances when your father died so unexpectedly in

1910. I've always felt badly that you and Ernest did not receive the same opportunities as your older siblings in that regard. It was the best I could do to feed, clothe, and keep a roof over our heads. I've always felt your sister Maude felt compelled to marry young, at the age of fifteen, so as not to be a burden.

Losing your father was dreadful. I don't know if you remember that he was ill with toothache for only a day or so before his life was taken from us. You were barely eleven, and Ernest barely eight when your father died. Family, friends, neighbors, and indeed, the whole town mourned the sudden loss. W.B., like his father, had been a well-respected fixture in the Gainesville community for years. Just as I pray you will never lose a child, I also pray you and Clarence will have a long and healthy life. It is devastating to lose the love of your life, as both my mother and I have experienced.

And so, life went on. You married, and Ernest was in the service; I felt relieved that my children were all settled. Marrying Mr. Shankles in Commerce was really an impulsive thing. We enjoyed each other's company, but I was lonely with all my children gone. It was unfortunate that he wanted more than just my company – he wanted what little money I had. I must confess I was not heartbroken when he died so suddenly. Nothing like when your father passed. I had always yearned to establish ties with my mother and siblings, so I made my way west, and I'm not ready to stop yet. I hope to make it out to California to see your older brother Charlie near San Francisco, Lord willing. Can you imagine an old Georgia woman like me in sunny California? Well, I hope I make it someday soon. I'd love to at least lay eyes on my little grandson Charles Clarke. He and your sister, Bessie Lucille, are the same age.

Tommie dear, this may be my last letter for some time. As I said before, I will be moving on soon and will wait to write when I have permanent residence. I hope my treatises have not tired you but I felt knowing my story might help you understand why I am away from my dear children and grandchildren. I do long to hear from you. Kiss those dear girls and take care of Clarence and yourself.

Always, your mother,

HHS

MY REFLECTION TWO

I knew my grandmother, Tommie. She and my grandfather, Clarence lived upstairs from us until she died when I was seven years old. We always called her "Mama," I suppose because our own mother called her that. I knew little about her life except the stories my own mama told me.

It's interesting that Tommie should have felt the same feelings of abandonment as her own mother. I know she and my own mother were close all their lives, proving the trend did not continue from mother to daughter indefinitely. I was far too young to observe my mother and grandmother's relationship to the point of understanding what it was like. However, memories my mother told me and some that my sister recalls are helpful in imagining how close it must have been. Will the next packet of letters reveal more?

Times have changed since I started reading the letters of my great-great and great-grandmothers to their daughters. Now, well into the nineteen hundreds and my own mother's existence, the art of letter writing is on the wane. The telephone has become the primary means of communication. The language used to put thoughts into words is more mundane, the subjects franker and more revealing, and the time between communication has shortened.

A small sense of unease creeps over me as I lift the next group of letters. Penciled on the first one is "Tommie and Mary." It is addressed to Mr. and Mrs.

Clarence Lord, Jefferson Hwy, Commerce, Georgia, and postmarked to Statham, Georgia. I knew my grandparents had lived in Commerce and that my mother had mostly grown up there. But Statham? I had never heard any reference to Statham and had no idea where it was. Looking at a map, I could see it was about forty miles southeast of Commerce.

I was holding in my hand envelopes my own mother and grandmother had held in theirs. Hands that held these letters had touched my cheek as a baby, wiped my tears, and sometimes had been raised in exasperation or imminent punishment. Would I learn something I didn't already know?

PART THREE

TOMMIE BELLE, MY GRANDMOTHER, AND MARY

MARY WRITES TO HER MOTHER, TOMMIE

Statham, Georgia
August 1939

Dear Mama,

I have news for you and Daddy. I know I told you I was going down to Statham to spend a few days with my friend LulaMae. That was partly true, but there is more to the story. I know times have been very lean for you and Daddy. Feeding a family of five has been a hardship. Now, with Christine married off and Lucille about to be, I need to tell you that I'm following them. This past Sunday, August 13th, I was married to Boyce Holliday. You've met him a few times. We are very much in love. I am making my home with his family in Statham for the time being. I hope you wish me well. I will visit soon. Write to me at the address on the outside of this envelope. Please take care of yourselves.

Your loving daughter,

Mary Lord Holliday

TOMMIE RESPONDS

Commerce, Georgia
September 1939

Dear Daughter,

Oh, my goodness. I hardly know what to say. My baby girl? Married? You are only fifteen years old! I appreciate you thinking of the hard times your daddy and I have, but I would not have wished for you to marry so young. You have always had a determined streak to do what you want, so I suppose there would have been no stopping you had we known. Daddy is not happy about this news either. Now that the deed is done, all we can do is wish you and Boyce the best. I'm sure his family has been experiencing hard times, too.

Y'all are welcome to visit anytime, but I suppose you will both be busy with farmwork. If you get too homesick, just come back. We will always take you in. I don't feel that I have prepared you for married life. I thought I would have at least a couple more years. There will be a baby coming along sometime next spring if there's not one already, and I know you are not prepared to be a mother. Oh well, enough about that.

Your Daddy and I are both in a bit of shock at your news. I will write again soon because I have much to tell you.

Yours,

Tommie Lord

Commerce, Georgia
October 1939

Dear Mary,

I haven't heard from you again since your letter telling us you were married. Hope you are doing all right down there in Statham. Do the Hollidays have a telephone? You could call over to Odell and Effie's next door some evening, and they could get me to come over and talk. If not, I guess letters will have to do until you get up here to Commerce for a visit. Daddy's about always home since he can't work, and I get home from the factory about five. We surely would love to see you. Bring Boyce along, too. After all, we're going to be family now.

You know I was eighteen when Clarence and I married. I also felt at the time like I was making it easier for my mother. Daddy had been gone eight years, and times had not been easy for my mother. Even though she took up with that other Smith fellow and Mr. Shankles, neither was a father to us, and both squandered what little money Mother had. My sisters eventually all married off, and she only had me and Ernest left at home. She had talked for years about wanting to go out to Texas to find her own Mother. When Ernest ran off and joined the Navy, I felt like I was the only thing holding Mother to Georgia.

Life was hard for her after my father died. She struggled to support those of us still at home. Teaching piano lessons did not bring in much income. It was an adjustment for all of us. We had never felt underprivileged in Gainesville, having been well-connected. Grandmother Permelia and my uncles made sure we never wanted for anything. That all changed after Mother moved to Commerce to make a new home with that other Mr. Smith. Things just never felt right with him around, so I was ready to leave, too. I will always remember that conversation I had with her when she talked about going to Texas.

"But Mama, I'm going to miss you!"

"I wouldn't expect you not to, darling Tommie Belle! But you are a grown woman now. You spend all your free time with that Clarence boy anyway. I hardly ever have an evening at home with you. With Ernest gone off to the Navy, it's quiet around here in the evenings." Mama seemed nonchalant about the whole thing.

"Well, Mama, I was going to talk to you about that. Clarence and I may be tying the knot soon."

"Oh, honey! That's wonderful. I could tell from the looks between you two things were getting serious. If that's what you want, I'm happy for you."

"Oh yes, Mama, it's what I want. But that doesn't mean I don't need you. I don't want you to go away!

"Oh, you'll manage well without me once you're married off. You'll start your own home, and babies will come along before you know it. Clarence has a big family, so you'll have plenty of kin folk around."

"Those are his people, Mama, not mine. My sisters are scattered all over, and my brothers are busy with their own lives. I won't know what to do without you."

"Ah, there you have it. Unlike when I was a young girl, you've had the advantage of a big family all through the years growing up. I've longed to get to know my sisters and brother my entire life. If I don't go soon, it may be too late. I never saw my father again after he left for Texas. Next thing I knew, he was dead and buried. I'd like to see my own mother at least once before she leaves this earth, too."

"Oh, Mama, I don't mean to be selfish, but I just can't imagine you being halfway across the country. Why, we talk every day, and you've always been here for me. What will I do with you gone?"

"Darling, you will do just fine. I vowed I would not leave my children

while they were young, as my mother and father did to me and Wade, and I have raised you all now, even after your father died, the best I knew how. I have no doubt you will do the same for your husband and family."

And that was that. There was no further discussion. Clarence and I had been friends for several months, and it wasn't a big leap for us to get married. I was eighteen, and he was nineteen, which about the average age for most folks around that time to get married. Less than a year later, your sister Christine was born. Lucille and you came over the next couple of years, and there I was, a married woman with three babies. My mother stayed long enough to see me married off, then left for Texas. I felt abandoned, just like my own mother had been. I wrote to her in Texas, begging her to come back to Georgia. She never did, but during that time is when she wrote all those letters telling me about her life.

I will make this promise to you. Although I will have to work for the remainder of my life, I will never abandon you or your sisters. I will do whatever I can to be there for you even though I'm so tired all the time from working in the heat at the overall factory. I have much more to tell you, but I must sign off now. Please write or call and let me know how you're getting along.

Mary, I love you and miss you so much.

Your Mama,

Tommie Lord

Commerce, Georgia
November 1939

Dear Mary,

I pray all is going well down there in Statham. Are they treating you well? I hope they don't think Boyce bringing home a young wife amounted to them gaining a farm hand or maid. Please let us know how you are doing. We are still adjusting to the idea that you are married off. It's hard to realize our baby girl is grown and gone.

Do you remember how you and your sisters played when you were just little bitty things? Your daddy doted on all of you, but you were his favorite. You don't need to tell Christine and Lucille that, but they know it anyway. Clarence nearly spent more time with you all since I worked most of the time, and he didn't. Then the others went off to school, and it was just you and him.

A couple of years after you were born at the tenant house in Hapeville, we moved closer to Atlanta out Utoy Road around 1927. Lucille and Christine started school at Utoy Springs Elementary, and you stayed home with Clarence while I worked at the shirt factory. He would take you on long walks, showing you the Civil War trenches. Sometimes, y'all would come home with a pocket full of bullet points and round balls. That was one thing your daddy loved to do. On some Sunday afternoons when I was home, he'd say, "Let's go ramble in the woods." I was never keen on doing that – I had too much work to do. I know you loved those times, even if all we had to eat were beans, greens, and cornbread. Sometimes, it was just the cornbread crumbled into the buttermilk – no beans or greens.

Little children don't usually realize just how poor or well-off their families are. As long as they have the necessities of life, love, and attention they don't pay any mind to anything else. When I was little and we lived in Gainesville, we weren't rich by any means, but we did all right. We were a huge family of ten children, and I was next to the youngest. It was always a bustling house. Grandparents, aunts, and uncles were always close by. We lived near town, and being well-known in the community meant friends and neighbors were always dropping in. Mama loved music, and we were always singing around the piano.

I'll never forget when my daddy died. I had just turned eleven. Daddy was never sick and never missed work at his job at the courthouse. He was always involved in politics and county business. Nobody realized when he died early that Sunday morning, May 8, 1910, that he had even been sick. He hadn't missed a day of work, going on to the courthouse the whole week before, even with his toothache. That turned out to be the death of him, as infection from the tooth abscess spread and was fatal. Mama knew it was serious, but the rest of us were shocked to wake that Sunday morning to the news that our father was dead.

I haven't forgotten you have a birthday coming soon. I know you think sixteen is grown up. But then you must have thought even fifteen was grown up enough to get married since you were still that when you decided to run off and get hitched. You always did have a mind of your own and thought you had to do everything your sisters did. Your Daddy always admired your spunk and encouraged you to be independent. I tended to see it more as a worry – and as it turns out now, I really do have something to worry about. There's not that much difference between fifteen and sixteen. Either one is young to be getting married and especially having a baby. It might be different if you were here where me and your sisters could look out for you. I'd feel so much better if you were close by.

Oh well, life sure does throw unexpected events at us sometimes. I could tell you more but will save some for another time. Mary, your Daddy and I miss you so much. Please let us know how you are faring down there. And don't forget if you want or need to come home, our door is always open.

Love you,

Your Mama

Commerce, Georgia
December 1939

Dear Mary,

I was so happy when you called last week. It was so good just to hear your voice. I wasn't surprised when you said you were pregnant. That's what naturally follows getting married. It was heartening to hear you say you'd been feeling well. I felt so poorly during the early months of expecting I feared you might be the same. I know we didn't get to talk long so I wanted to write and tell you more of what I wanted to say.

When I was a young mother and had you and your sisters, your daddy was not much help, and I had no family around. My Mama had taken off to Texas. Clarence worked from time to time, but after his fingers got cut off at the factory, he never really wanted to go back to that kind of full-time job. He'd take on little jobs for folks, do some tenant farming, that kind of thing. You might remember when you were just a little bitty thing, we moved around a lot, and that was why. We had to go wherever we would have a roof over our heads and food to eat. Sometimes down around Atlanta, and one time even in South Georgia. When the overall factory opened in Commerce, we came here, and I was our main source of income. At least we were able to stay in one place and were closer to the Lords, even if I no longer had any family around. I didn't take too kindly having to depend on myself to bring in what little money we had, but I did what I had to do to take care of you and your sisters.

This is one thing I want you to know now that you're starting off in a marriage of your own. It would have been better if I could have told you all this before, but that's water under the bridge now. I hope and pray it all works out for you and Boyce, and you won't have the hard life I had when I was a young mother and still have to this day. It's important to have a husband who will support you and any children you have. Lord willing, you won't have to toil as I do for long hours in unbearable conditions. Law, some days I think my back will break before I can finish my hours and get home. There's no relief there either – there's supper to get and your daddy to deal with.

Well, that's enough of my complaining. I know you said on the telephone you helped some down there on their farm. Hopefully, they won't work you too hard now the days of harvesting are close to over, and especially with you pregnant. I was sorry to hear Boyce's mother was feeling poorly. That's an untimely circumstance for you, having to feed the father, mother, husband, his brothers, and a farmhand. Surely, she will be back on her feet soon. Please take care of yourself. You're so young to have so much responsibility and pregnant, too. Having a baby at your age can be difficult, and I want to be sure you are being seen after properly. You should go to the doctor and make sure everything is all right.

Sorry if I sound like I'm fussing at you, but I suppose that is what I'm doing. Mary, it broke mine and your Daddy's heart for you to go off like that without a hint of what you were planning. Truthfully, not only were we heartbroken, but we were angry with you at first. Now that we know you are expecting, we've gotten over being mad, but we do worry about you. I apologize if I'm being too frank with you about all this, but you have made your choice, and now you'll have to live with it. Married life may not be turning out like you thought. If at any time you feel like you need to come home, you will always be welcome.

Do you remember how I told you about missing my mother after she went to Texas? I felt so alone. At least you are just down the highway. I never dreamed when my mother left, right after your daddy and I married, that I would never lay eyes on her again. When I got the telegram that she had passed away, I couldn't believe it. She was only sixty-five. She would never see my baby girls, but she did manage to see those grandsons out in California. My older brothers and sisters had her brought back to Georgia to bury her beside my father, but I still felt abandoned. Your Daddy and I couldn't contribute anything for the expenses. Although Ernest and I stay in touch, I only hear from others occasionally, usually when somebody marries, dies, or has a baby.

I say all this so you will know I don't want our family to end up like that. Your daddy and I always want to be a part of your life and know our grandchildren. We want your sisters to stay close. Hopefully, your children can be close too. I wish I had known my extended family better. Oh well, enough about me and my regrets.

Do remember, we love you. Please call again soon or come for a visit at least. Christmas is coming soon, and although it will be meager, I would love to have you home. Boyce could come too, if you'd like. Lucille and Christine will both be here. I would love to have all my girls here together.

Your loving mother,

Tommie Belle

Commerce, Georgia
January 1940

Dear Mary,

It was good to see you and Boyce on Christmas Day, even if the visit was short. This letter may not be long, but there are some serious thoughts your father and I want to tell you about. After the two of you left, your sisters told us they were so worried about you. You just didn't seem to be the happy, carefree girl you were only a few months ago. You were pale and spoke very little. Boyce was nice enough, but there wasn't much on conversation. If we didn't know you were expecting, we could never tell from your appearance. You don't look as if you've even gained a pound! At five months, you should begin to show a little.

Mary, we implore you to come home to us. We can't know what's going on at the Hollidays, but something just doesn't feel right. We are all worried about you and the health of your baby. We need to get you to a doctor. Things might be tight here, but I'm sure it's tight there, too, and there are more of them than there would be here with Daddy, me, you, and Lucille. Do whatever you need to do to come back to us. If you need money, we will scrape some together and find a way to get it to you. If you need a way, we will find somebody to come for you.

I don't know how much you've been in touch with your sisters, but they both have news to share as well. Although it is early, I will become a grandmother not once, not twice, but three times in the coming year! Christine and Alston are happy, but I fear Lucille and her fellow, Clifford, may not make a home. Both being only eighteen, and him living with his folks, and Lucille here, does not bode well. At least you and Boyce are married and living together. I never had the opportunity to be with my own sisters or even my own mother in my early married years. I would have loved to have had that opportunity.

The older I get, the more I appreciate the importance of family. I suppose that comes from my own fractured experience, and I wish it could be dif-

ferent for my girls. It may take an effort, but it will be well worthwhile. With the talk of war, I have concerns for the young men. Best to take advantage of any times we can all be together.

Please call or write as soon as possible and let us know if you will consider coming home. We love you.

Your Mother,

Tommie Belle

Commerce, Georgia
February 1940

Dear Mary,

I truly hoped we would hear from you with the news that you were coming home after my last letter, but you are determined to do things your way, as always. We are so worried about you. I've fussed and complained, and it doesn't seem to make any difference. You are your Daddy's daughter when it comes to stubbornness.

Let me think and see if I can come up with something more pleasant to tell you about. Your Daddy and I don't go to church much these days. After working all week, it's all I can do to get the laundry, canning, and other household chores done on Sundays. When we were younger and just starting out, church was one of the places we often saw each other. I'd been raised Methodist; my father and grandfather were both prominent men in the Methodist Church in Gainesville. After leaving Gainesville, I mostly went to the Dry Pond Church in Commerce. Your Daddy went to the Blacks Creek Baptist Church where his Mama and Daddy had gone until she died in 1914. Those little country churches were so sweet and different from the big city church in Gainesville. Your Daddy started coming over to the Methodist Church with me when I could talk him into it, and that's where we took you young'uns when we lived around there. After that, I tried to find a Methodist Church close by wherever we lived. It needed to be within walking distance. Your Daddy never was much for going to church, and we didn't have an automobile. Getting three little girls and myself gussied up for church was quite a chore, but I tried to make sure I did right with the three of you. I know you don't care for church much these days, but I hope you will take your child. When times are hard, church can be a comfort.

Oh dear, I've been rambling. I didn't mean to preach to you. Heaven knows I've made my mistakes. I had hoped so much and prayed you'd have an easier time of it than I did. Being a young wife and mother with little family support is not an easy task. You are strong and independent, and I'm sure you will do fine.

Know that your Daddy and I love you and will always be here for you. It's looking like we will have Lucille and her baby with us indefinitely once it arrives. That worthless thing she took up with has not taken the slightest interest in making a home for them, although there are still a few months to go. Christine and Alston are making a go of it, and their baby is due around the same time as Lucille's. But you will have my first grandchild in just a few short weeks! Should you decide to come back to us, we will gladly take you and the baby in, too. We've been thinking about making a move to Atlanta. There are better jobs there, and maybe even your Daddy could find something. Wherever we are, you and the baby will always be welcome.

Your loving Mama,

Tommie Belle

MARY RESPONDS TO HER MOTHER, TOMMIE

Statham, Georgia
March 1940

Dear Mama,

I have been giving some thought to coming home. Your last letter has helped me decide to do just that. I've never felt at home here with the Hollidays. I know Boyce won't be happy about it, but I must think of myself and this baby. Even if we end up going to Atlanta, that will be fine, too. It might be nice to live in the big city for a change. I don't care about farm life! Maybe Lucille and me can help each other out with the babies. Anyway, I'll let you know when I can get home, but I'll tell you this. It won't be soon enough for me.

Love,

Your daughter, Mary

MY REFLECTION THREE

Sad, so sad. I'd often heard my mother talk about the hard life her own mother had, but there were never any details. Occasionally, she would mention times during the Depression when they barely had enough to eat. I knew they'd lived in Commerce, and we had even driven up to see the graves of relatives at the Dry Pond and Blacks Creek churches.

Would the letter box reveal more stories? Only one more packet remained. I had read the letters written from 1903 up to 1940, and the number of letters from mother to daughter had decreased with time. It had started with Harriet writing to express her bitterness towards her mother and father, who left her behind when they relocated to Texas after the Civil War. My great-great-grandmother Adeline had written eleven letters responding to her daughter Harriet throughout 1903-1904. After Harriet's daughter Tommie wrote to Harriet in 1923 expressing her own feelings of abandonment, Harriet wrote a series of eight letters back to her in 1924 before passing away in Texas, never having seen Tommie again or her three granddaughters. In 1939, when my mother, Mary, wrote to her mother, Tommie, announcing she had run off and married, Tommie's six letters revealed how heartbroken she was over her youngest daughter's actions. I knew my mother had returned to her parents before Tommy was born. She had told me once when I asked about it that she and Boyce never really had a home of their own.

Now, there remained just one more packet. Not nearly so tattered as the others, this bundle was thinner and almost appeared brand-new. As I untied the ribbon, I saw there was no postmark! The flowing script across the top letter read "From Mary to Janet." Oh my God. My mother and I sometimes had a rocky relationship. What would these letters reveal? Would there be surprises? Would I find explanations for some of the hurtful exchanges we'd had? Would I find remorse, forgiveness, or even possibly vengefulness? I had not written to my mother expressing bitterness as the other daughters had. Had she sensed what I had left unspoken?

I hesitated to open the first envelope. Did I really want to know what was inside? At this point, my mother had been gone for almost twenty-five years. Did I want to open old wounds? Or could there, perhaps, be a balm to soothe the past hurts? There was only one way to find out. With trembling fingers, I lifted the top letter and slipped my finger under the seal.

PART FOUR

MARY, MY MOTHER, TO ME

Atlanta, Georgia
October 1968

Dear Janet,

I don't know when or if you will ever read this letter and the ones to follow, but I feel I must write it anyway. We don't seem to have the kind of relationship where I could say these words aloud. First, I love you with all my heart and will always be here for you, even if you find that hard to believe. Now that you are fifteen, I want to tell you a few things about life, my life. I want better for you than what I ever had. You are on the verge of womanhood and will be making many decisions over the next few years. I know at your age, girls don't listen to their mothers. You think we don't know anything relevant to your life. You, especially, are so reticent and don't share your thoughts or feelings. You keep things bottled up inside. It doesn't seem like you and I are very close; I don't know why. I wonder sometimes if that is my fault. Was it because I was always working? Did I not give you enough love and attention? Did we not have enough mother-daughter talks? Why, I remember you didn't even tell me when you started your periods when you were thirteen! I can't dwell on that right now; it might help you to know something about my life.

I had nothing when I was fifteen. My first husband, Boyce, turned my head. I suppose I loved him in my own way, but I just wanted out of the mundane life in a poor mill town. I gave no thought to any possible long-term effects of running away to get married. I soon discovered farm life with Boyce and his family was not for me. I had Tommy to take care of and no help from Boyce or his family of men. When Mama and Daddy decided to leave Commerce and move to Atlanta in search of better work, I didn't have to think twice –I was going with them.

Boyce showed up a few times, begging me to come home, but the attraction of Atlanta offered a life better than that of being a dirt-poor farmer's wife in a little rural place like Statham. Movies, clubs, people, and restaurants were all part of a world I'd never even known existed.

Mama and Daddy both went to work right away, her at the shirt factory and him selling papers. Lucille and her baby, Anne, were with us, too, after she gave up on Clifford ever settling down. After we got the babies to bed at night, we were able to feel young and free as we got to know the nightlife of Atlanta. We were young, still teenagers, and although we had babies at home, we had no husbands to speak of. It might not sound so good, but at least Tommy and Anne were with our own Mama and Daddy. Times were different back then. We were just beginning to get over the Depression, war was brewing, money was flowing, and life seemed full of possibilities. That's when I met your daddy.

I'm going to put this letter away for now. I'm not sure that I will ever actually pass it along to you, but I feel better just for having written down these things. I want you to have carefree young years. Life won't always be that way, but make the most of it while you can. There's so much for parents to worry about these days, what with drugs, riots, hippies, free love, protests, and all that nonsense. I know how much you love your church activities, and I'm glad you do, but that doesn't offer any guarantees. And this boy you're so wild about – I hate to see you so wrapped up in just him. I'm not so old to have forgotten what it's like to be given attention. I don't care about the way he treats you. You deserve better. I don't want to sound like I'm fussing, so I'm going to stop for now. There's much more I want to say, so I will write again.

Love,

Your Mother

Atlanta, Georgia
(undated)

Dear Janet,

Hello. First, let me tell you again that I love you and am proud of you. I know our family wasn't the type to show affection or tell you in words, but that doesn't mean Daddy and I didn't love all of you or were proud of your accomplishments. When you were little, you were always well-behaved and did well in school. I guess I thought, at least I didn't have to worry about you or expend any time or energy making sure you were doing what you were supposed to.

I know now that sounds lame. I remember, as a little girl, you saying how you wanted to be an artist, a movie star, an interior designer, and all kinds of exciting things like that. I told you, "People like us" didn't get to be things like that, and you could be a teacher or a nurse. I remember the puzzled look on your face. I would give anything if I could take those words back. I was only trying to protect you from disappointment. I knew we didn't have the money for fancy schools. We were a working-class family.

Part of that reality was based on my own experience. Let me go back and tell you a little more about my life. It might help you understand what made me sound harsh at times. I told you before about coming to Atlanta with my Mama and Daddy at only sixteen and with a baby and no physically present husband. Those were the circumstances when I met your Daddy.

My sister Lucille and I would often go out at night. There were several movie theatres and little bars within walking distance of where we lived on Lee Street, and we liked to go out and see movies when we could scrape up the money and have a beer. Age was not a big deal in those days. There would be jukeboxes playing and plenty of men hanging around, too. Yes, I met your daddy in a bar. When this fellow approached me, I swear I thought I was seeing a movie star. He had black hair, a swagger, and a crooked smile and was the perfect likeness to Humphrey Bogart.

We hit it off and started seeing each other on a regular basis. Mama and Daddy weren't crazy about the situation. I was still barely seventeen and still married to Boyce. Jimmy was twenty-seven and had an ex-wife and a seven-year-old daughter. It did not look like the most promising relationship in their eyes, and I can understand that now. But I was in love, and Jimmy professed to love me, and he was willing to take on a young woman with a baby. I'm sure his crazy mother wasn't thrilled, either. November of 1941 turned into an eventful month. My divorce from Boyce came through on the thirteenth, your daddy and I got married on the fifteenth, and I turned eighteen on the seventeenth! We were young and in love, Jimmy had a decent job, and life seemed good for a time. Little did we know then that by next November, he would be miles away, I'd be back on my own with my Mama and Daddy, and I'd have another baby.

Janet, when you're young, it seems like love is all that matters. We look at the world through the proverbial rose-colored glasses. Then life throws rocks in your direction and shatters those glasses until you feel like you're stumbling blindly in a fog of worries. I know I can't protect you from all of life's problems, but oh my darling, I would give anything if only I could prevent some heartaches from coming your way.

I do love you and want only for your happiness in life. I will write more soon as there is much more I want to tell you.

Love,

Your Mother

Atlanta, Georgia
(undated)

Dear Janet,

I know you are a smart girl. You get good grades, and so far, you haven't gotten into any trouble, at least not any that I know of. But sometimes, when a girl is young and gets so wrapped up in a boy, it's easy to make decisions that affect your entire life. I should know! You keep things to yourself so much, but I can see how you feel about this boyfriend. I also see that he does not treat you well. I'm afraid if I say too much against him, you will love him more fiercely, so I'm trying to keep my mouth shut. I can only hope and pray things don't get out of hand. Lord, Lord, all the things a mother and father have to worry about these days!

Let me tell you a little more about my life when I was eighteen. When your Daddy and I got married, he had already registered for the draft – all the men had to starting in the fall of 1940. The Germans were taking over Europe, but President Roosevelt was reluctant to get the US involved. That all changed when Japan bombed our base in Pearl Harbor on December 7, 1941, less than a month after we married. We knew then it was only a matter of time until every able-bodied man would be called up. Your Daddy enlisted in the army on April 6, 1942.

When he left, we had no idea where he was going or how long. Even the mail was censored. I'd get letters that had been opened, read, and cleared. I lived with Mama and Daddy and was pregnant with Sandra when he left. It was a terrible time. Being in the army, I never thought he would be in the Pacific, so I wasn't worried about that. I could glean from his letters his location as he was moved around and could tell he wasn't in combat in Europe either, so that was a bit of relief, but we never could be sure. Meanwhile, life at home was tough. I thought it had been bad during the Depression, but war rationing was strict, so many goods were just not available. We knew we wouldn't starve and got payments from the Army, but we were all in it together. There was medical care for wives and dependent children – a good thing since I was pregnant. Families stuck close, and folks did whatever they could to help the war effort. It's not easy being the one left behind, especially with two babies at home. Jimmy had really taken to Tommy, but Boyce showed up from time to time, wanting to see him. We rarely heard from Jimmy's first wife or saw his daughter, Nancy, but I know he got dependent payments for her, too, that were passed on to them. That was fine with me – I didn't want anything to do with either of them.

Oh, Janet, I pray you will never have to send a husband off to war. It's a terrible thing to fear losing your love every moment of your life. I wish your life could be happy and carefree, but that's unlikely. Life doesn't work that way. One day, you will understand that parents always want the best for their children and would take their burdens from them if they could. Daddy and I both love you and want all the happiness in the world for you. For now, you need to finish school and get some direction for your life, even if there's no man involved. Having a husband doesn't guarantee a life of leisure. Lord knows I had a good one in your daddy, but I've also worked hard all my life so all of you kids could have it better than I did. I suppose that's enough for now –

Love,

Your Mama

Atlanta, Georgia
September 1970

Dear Janet,

Reading back on what I've written, I don't know that it conveys the sentiment I'm trying to share with you. You are young still, just barely out of school. I know you are mature for your age, and the world is a different place these days, but I feel like you've been sheltered in many ways. That's about to change as you go to college. I can't tell you how proud we are that this is happening to you. Daddy and I always wanted more for all our kids but never dreamed we'd actually send one to college!

Of course, we were proud of all of you. It took Sandra a while to adjust to Daddy after he got out of the army in June of 1945. It was a grim time – they went ahead and let him discharge when the baby girl was stillborn, but he wasn't home yet.

That is another thing I hope and pray you will never have to experience. I'd gotten pregnant when he was home on leave, and it all was going well. The doctors offered no explanation for why she was stillborn. In those days, we didn't have all the tests and precautions that are available now. In those days, we weren't awake during childbirth, so I don't really remember anything but the aftermath. I was told she was a beautiful, perfectly formed baby girl, and it was best for me to just get over it and move on. Huh. Easy for them to say. A mother never gets over losing a baby. They kept me pretty doped up, so I was in a daze for weeks afterward. Granny made all the arrangements for the baby to be buried next to Daddy's daddy in the plots she had at Greenwood.

Daddy got home that summer, and the country celebrated the end of the war with the bombings of Japan. At the time, I don't think any of us understood the gravity of nuclear bombs. We were happy the war was over and life could move on. I was pregnant again within weeks, Daddy got back to work, and we had a happy life with friends and family. It was like the stillbirth and the war had never happened.

Over the years, there have been moments when I think of those days and wonder how we were able to move on so easily. It seems like those kinds of life events would have absolutely devastating effects, and they did for some, or maybe we just never recognized them in our own lives. In those times, people didn't dwell on their problems. We just went on with our lives.

Well, I didn't mean to get so morbid here. Who knows what life will hold for you in the future? I can only hope and pray your future will hold much happiness. That is what parents wish for their children. I love you, baby girl.

–Your Mama

Atlanta, Georgia
1971

Dear Janet,

It's been a while since I've written. I don't know if you will ever read these letters, but I suspect that at some point, perhaps many years after I'm dead and gone, you will do so. I don't intend for you to read them before then, but I still feel better for having written what I find difficult to say to you in person. It makes me sad that we've never had that kind of relationship, although I know that much of the blame is my own.

Let me tell you more about our family life. Those years after the war were good for us. Although life was hectic with three little ones, we had grand times. There were plenty of babysitters, with Mama and Granddaddy just upstairs, and Lucille and Dorsey across the street. It was an idyllic time in West End. We lived just around the corner from the American Legion Post, and it was our social hub. Daddy was a commander, and there was always something going on – dances, parties, bingo, and the clandestine slot machines and poker games. Nobody really cared that the veterans and their families were celebrating – it was thought they deserved every right to have a good life. We would occasionally go downtown to party, and life was good. We had a brief scare in the fifties when the war in Korea cranked up. The last thing I wanted was for Jimmy to have to go back to the service and leave me with three children at home. We'd been lucky in the previous war, but that didn't mean we were safe. Thankfully, it played out before the men over forty with dependents were called up. All seemed well, and we were moving on with our lives.

It was late January of 1953 when I began to suspect. At first, I thought I had the flu. But then it became obvious it was more than that. I was pregnant. Tommy was twelve, Sandra was ten, and Mike was seven. All big enough to be self-sufficient. The last thing I wanted was another baby. In those days, we didn't really plan babies; we were just aware of the calendar and hoped for the best. I thought my family was set, and I was just beginning to enjoy some independence. Daddy had a decent job, and we were managing financially, if not rolling in dough. I moped and cried to my Mama, who offered little sympathy. She only harumphed and said, "Well, you know what causes it."

It may sound harsh to admit your arrival was not happily anticipated, but as I've said before, that's just the way life was in those days. I resolved to make the best of it. After you were born, you were doted on by everybody. There was an extended family all around; Sandra was old enough to babysit, Jimmy was home at night, and I was able to start working. Working shifts at National Biscuit Company and then Owens-Illinois wasn't so bad. It got me out of the house, the extra money was nice, and I made friends. Little did I realize the lifelong precedent I was setting.

The real kicker came about four years later when I found myself pregnant again. Having a baby at the age of thirty-five! Oh hell. My fate was truly sealed now. I gave little thought to the idea of not working. After all, it wasn't really an option by that point. It wasn't cheap to maintain a family of five kids. Three teenagers and two little ones took every penny Daddy and I could earn and then some. As another decade approached and 1960 loomed, all our lives would soon change as never before.

Janet, it's a blessing in disguise that children are often oblivious to the turmoil going on around them. It affects their lives, but thankfully, they usually don't realize the seriousness of some of life's circumstances. Those situations do, however, cause their parents to behave in ways that I now know are less than ideal. At the time, we were doing the best we knew how without regard for any long-term damage that might result. That's all most parents can do.

Oh, Janet, I have many regrets about your growing-up years. All I can do is hope and pray you will forgive me. None of the hurts were ever intended, but I know that doesn't ease the pain. I know they have left scars that have prevented us from being as close as I would like. Perhaps time can help heal some of the wounds.

That's enough for now. It's painful for me to remember and admit these mistakes. I will write more, and hopefully, we can find some peace together.

Love,

Your Mother

Atlanta, Georgia
(undated)

Dear Janet,

There is no way I could have told you about these things in person. I pray that when you do get to read these letters you will find it in your heart to forgive me. It was not until years after you were grown that I realized the damaging effects of distancing myself from you and Randy through work as if the sixties didn't offer enough other distractions. You would think losing my own dear Mama in sixty-one would have made me stop and think, but I was more determined than ever to work hard to provide for our family.

At the time, I told myself I didn't really have a choice. We built the new house on Venetian in 1960, and I thought I had died and gone to heaven. A modern brick house with built-in kitchen cabinets and a bath and a half. That was only made possible because Granny gave us the lot and helped with the money. I made good money, and Daddy did okay, but his health problems plagued him, and he was often out of work. Tommy and Sandra both married and were on their own. Mike was nearing graduation and had hopes of going to college on a football scholarship. College! Daddy and I never dreamed our children would go to college, but suddenly, it seemed like a real possibility. Then Granny died in sixty-three, Mike didn't take to college, the war in Vietnam escalated, and all hell broke loose as the Black people started taking over. The second half of the sixties brought one crisis after another.

That left just you and Randy, both in grammar school. You never gave us any worries – making straight A's, being a teacher's pet, and wanting to participate in everything. It was actually frustrating because every time you won an award, I'd be expected to show up at school, or had to provide a costume for some special program, or just say no, you couldn't do something because there was no way to get you back and forth to extra-curricular activities with me working shifts. Still, you managed to thrive. Randy, not so much. He was always in trouble. He was determined to get attention any way he could, even if it was the wrong kind.

Daddy did his part and would take you back and forth to church, on work errands with him, and got y'all to bed or up for school when I was working. That church business was another story. I'd never been much of a churchgoer, and when I was younger, we grew up going to the Methodist church. I didn't have much use for Baptists. I didn't mind you being involved so much, but those other girls' mamas thought they were so high and mighty and better than me. They'd come to visit and look down their noses at us. I only put up with it because I knew how much you loved it. I never gave it any thought how hard it must have been for you – the only little girl of the bunch whose parents never attended. I know that as you got older, you realized the differences.

Janet, I'm sorry I never told you how proud I was of all your accomplishments. I know we were never openly affectionate. I guess in family life those days, we just assumed you knew we loved you and were proud of you. After all, it was expected that children would behave and do well, and we provided for your needs. My work made it possible to buy you faddish clothes and the John Romain purses and pay for you to go on church trips. In my mind, at that time, I thought it was enough. Sadly, I now know that was not the case.

I suppose if you're reading these letters, you've also read the others going all the way back from my great-grandmother to my grandmother. It's interesting that Harriet and Tommie Belle felt feelings of abandonment. I never felt that way, but I can see how my work was a form of neglect in its own way, at least for you and Randy. Your striving for recognition must have been your own way of seeking praise and attention you didn't get at home. I thank God that despite my lack of involvement in your life, you have done well.

I do love you, Janet, and know that you love me in your own way. God knows I didn't provide the greatest example, and I have only myself to blame for that. I will write again and talk about how you came into your own as a young woman and how proud of you Daddy and I both were.

Love forever,

Your Mother

Atlanta, Georgia
(undated)

Dear Janet,

As I look back on your high school years in the last half of the 1960s, it all seems like a blur. I often wonder if it seemed the same for you. There was so much going on. We worried to death about hippies and the drug culture, although I didn't think you would seriously fall into that. But you did seem all into the peace and love movement, so we couldn't be sure. I was mostly preoccupied with Daddy's health – he was in and out of hospital with his arteries and eye problems – do you remember that?

Even more than that was the year Mike was in Vietnam. Every night on the TV news were clips of soldiers, death, and destruction. It hadn't been like that when Daddy was in the service or even during Korea, but seeing bombs and shooting right in front of our eyes was a horror story. I know you were part of the generation that didn't agree with our being in Vietnam, and confidentially, I didn't either. It was a no-win situation. But I would fiercely defend the war because my son was there. I pray you will never know the pain of knowing one of your children is in that kind of danger and could be taken from you at any point. All we could do was pray for God's protection.

There were also civil rights issues causing fears and concerns. When you started high school, it was the first time you went to school with Black people. There were fears of riots and uprisings when Martin Luther King Jr. was assassinated. Atlanta was changing as white flight started to decimate our beloved West End and surrounding areas. Almost worse than the fear of violence was the fear you might have Black friends or – horrors – a Black boyfriend! You seemed nonchalant about race issues, but then, my mind was mostly on other things, so I didn't give your thoughts or opinions a lot of credence.

Of course, I still wanted you to have it better than I had. I feared your seriousness over certain boyfriends. I could see how heartbroken you were over broken dates or being stood up, and my heart ached for you. I knew how crazy in love you were with that one boy, but I just did not like the way he treated you. The last thing I wanted was for you to end up like I did – pregnant. I felt like your church involvement was somewhat of a safeguard where that was concerned, but I knew from experience it was no guarantee.

By some miracle, you neared the end of high school safely and soundly. It was unexpected when you came up with the idea in the spring of 1970 of skipping your senior year and graduating early. Daddy and I weren't so sure about it, but you insisted things were so bad at school that you'd be better off getting out. The only dilemma was, what would you do? You always got good grades, and deep down inside, Daddy and I thought if we could find a way, you should go to college, but we always thought there would be another year to plan for that. There was no way we could afford to send you off to school. And you yourself really had no idea what you wanted to do, except for saying you'd like to work with kids. You enjoyed that at church.

Once you got it into your head that you were going to attend summer school, graduate early, and skip your senior year, there was no stopping you. I remember you saying you'd just find a job, get an apartment with a girlfriend, and that would be that. I wasn't crazy about that plan. I knew you had the potential for more than just clerking in a store or being a secretary. When I saw the little article in the newspaper about the new Pediatric Assistant Program at Georgia State, I thought it sounded like a possibility. When you agreed to at least go talk to the woman in charge, I was relieved. Somehow, we made it all work out. We rushed around and got you enrolled, and by September, you were out of high school, still living at home and going to college!

Again, I don't know whether Daddy or I ever told you how proud we were – a child of ours in college! Mike was home, your boyfriend situation seemed to be resolving, and now we just had Randy to get through high school. Life went on, and we made the best of things.

Janet, I know we never told you, but you were our shining star. You were opinionated, and we didn't always agree on things, but your independent streak would serve you well. Daddy especially enjoyed carrying on intelligent conversations with you. He wasn't very formally educated, but he read and was knowledgeable on many subjects. I think military experience and seeing at least some of the world made that difference for him, just as it did for Mike. College was doing the same for you.

The next few years would bring so many changes. You were nearly grown, even if you had rushed things a bit. I prayed it would all work out well for you; for the most part, it seemed to. We would have some rocky times, but overall, I think we have come to terms with our differences. Maybe one or two more letters can sum up our relationship and bring closure for both of us.

Love you always,

Mother

Atlanta, Georgia
(undated)

Dear Janet,

Looking back on it now, it seems like the next few years went by in the blink of an eye. That could be because of my disengagement, but I know you will find that time does appear to go by more quickly as you get older. You were busy with school, dating, and working odd jobs here and there.

During those years, I felt like I could be pretty much hands-off. I no longer worried about drugs, hippies, or any of that. Your boy-craziness had seemed to settle down a bit. Still, I had concerns when you started seeing Joe. Even though he was a boy you knew from church, that didn't offer me much reassurance. After all, you were barely eighteen, and he was twenty-seven! You were still just a girl, albeit already a sophomore in college. You still had a year to go to graduate your program. Add to that that, he had motorcycles, two cars, and lived in his own apartment! He wasn't in college, hadn't gone to college, but did have a job in data processing, a whole new field Daddy and I knew nothing about. I couldn't say a whole lot, considering your Daddy was eleven years older than me, and I was only seventeen when we got married. Once y'all were engaged and determined to get married, I had to accept it. Daddy took to Joe and liked him a lot. It took a while for me to come to appreciate Joe's qualities. As it turned out, he was the best thing that ever happened to you, although I did think it would be good for you to experience some independence before settling down and getting married. I knew you were in for some big surprises with married life, but I never realized just how big those surprises would be until many years later.

Just like always, you never shared much about your personal life with me. You weren't even very close to your sister Sandra. I suppose the age difference was the cause of that. Sometimes, I could sense that all was not as perfect as it appeared to be, but true to our own relationship, I kept my distance and didn't interfere. I know you had some good friends with whom you confided, but your fierce stoicism stood firm, and you soldiered on through whatever inner unrest was smoldering.

I know you took it hard when Daddy died. I remember telling you at the hospital that day that you had always been his favorite. I wasn't sure if you knew that, but I thought you deserved to know. I'm sure you have romanticized that notion over the years, but it really was true. As they say, women often marry someone like their father, and it became increasingly clear over the years how much Joe was like your Daddy. How I wish he had lived longer – I think they would have been great friends. Did you realize I was only fifty years old when Daddy died? I know that must have seemed ancient to you at the time. I was still working full time, Randy was still a year from graduating high school, and the rest of you were on your own. I never talked about going through that, and maybe I should have, but it was like so much in my life and yours. We didn't dwell on things – we just kept on keeping on. I regret that we never truly shared our feelings on so many life events until it was too late.

After your babies came along and times were financially tough for y'all, I worried but kept my thoughts to myself. I hated to see y'all struggling, but I had to be careful about trying to "help." I had come to really love Joe and didn't want to hurt his pride, and I also didn't want to appear to play favorites, so I resorted to my default position – hands off. I hope you didn't think I was just being cold-hearted, but that was the way our relationship had always been, and I didn't see it changing in the near future.

I know this letter has been shorter than most, but it still tells the story of what our lives were like during those days. I will try to sum up the last chapter of our lives together in a final letter –

Love,

Your Mother

Riverdale, Georgia
1995

Dear Janet,

This may be the most difficult of all these letters to write. It's interesting to think about now, but I don't really remember us deciding to live together, do you? It seems like the idea just seemed to evolve. Y'all had been through some tough times and decided to move back to the south side of town to be near the airport for Joe's work. It was becoming clear that it wasn't safe for me to live alone in the house on Venetian. Somehow, we decided to buy a house together, and I would have my own space to live with y'all and have a home for the rest of my life.

I remember saying something to the effect that it wouldn't be for too long. I think I was around sixty-three at the time. My mother had died at only sixty-two, and I didn't expect to live much longer than that myself, so I thought I could go at any time. Y'all pooh-poohed that idea, considering the medical advances that had taken place over the years. Anyway, I never dreamed it would be almost fifteen years of living our lives together.

So much happened during those years. Your boys were growing up. Joe's job at the airlines remained precarious. You were working at the big Baptist Church in Jonesboro, supposedly part-time, but it seemed more like full-time. Y'all were there every time the doors were open. You were also leading workshops all over. You had become a leader in your field of ministry education, although I never quite understood what it was all about. I kind of hated that you weren't using your pediatric education from years before, but you defended that, saying it had provided the foundation of your knowledge for child development. I still sensed that you wanted to do more but just couldn't figure out how to get there. I tried to be as much help as I could without interfering, especially with the boys and financially.

I know you were under a great deal of stress when Joe had to work out of town during some of those strike days, but as always, my entire life,

I'd had to struggle, and we just did whatever we had to do. We didn't wallow in self-pity. Not to say that you did that, but holding in your emotions is not healthy either. Sometimes, I felt like you used your work as an escape, just like I did. I also know times had changed, but I wasn't convinced that it was normal for families to not sit down for dinner together every night, eat on the run, and be on the go all the time. But then, I never knew what it was to cart three boys to ball practices and ball games every evening and every Saturday, either. I know sometimes my comments were pretty pointed in questioning your mothering and your housekeeping (what there was of it). Looking back, it's surprising you didn't defend yourself. True to your usual behavior, you took it all in without lashing out.

There did come a time eventually when you'd let slip snide little comments here and there. I supposed that was your passive-aggressive way of getting back at me. Do you remember the one night when it all kind of came to a head? We had been at Sandra's for a family cookout. Something came up in conversation about how I was known to speak my mind without much consideration for the feelings of others. Now, I must admit to being guilty of that. And the older I got, the more I felt entitled to say whatever I thought. Your comment at the time, however, floored me. You said, "Yep. Try living with that twenty-four-seven for years on end!" Nobody seemed shocked, and we all laughed it off. I let it slide for the moment, but it got under my skin.

Later that night, back at home, I called you down to my room. I said, "Sit down; we need to talk."

"Okay. What's up?"

"Do you want me to move out?"

"What? What are you talking about? Who said anything about moving out?"

"Well, what you said tonight about living with me twenty-four-seven

for years on end made me think. It's obvious you are not happy with our arrangement. You barely speak to me when you come home every day. You ignore most of my attempts at conversation or argue and disagree. Something is not right here."

"But Mama, I have to talk to people all day! A whole classroom of them! When I get home, all I want is a little peace and quiet. Is that so terrible?"

I know you may recall this conversation differently, but this is my version.

Then you said, "No! Move out? Of course not! What makes you think that?"

"Well, as I said, your little comments here and there and the way you speak to me with what feels like disdain. Why, Joe is more civil to me than you are. You'd think he was the son, and you were the in-law!"

"Oh, Mom, that's just the way I get sometimes. I will say this – I don't get positive feelings from you either. In fact, I never have. It seems like all you do is criticize. I never do anything right. According to you, I'm a terrible mother, an awful housekeeper, and an ungrateful daughter. Even when I was a little girl, you never said you were proud of me, that you loved me, or encouraged me. In fact, you acted annoyed if you had to attend some special event or pay for something extra. It was always like I was just one big inconvenience. Nothing I can do is ever good enough for you. It gets old hearing that all the time."

At this point, the tears began to flow, yours and mine both. "Oh, Janet, I've always been proud of you! And I do love you. I know that it wasn't ever expressed in words, but we made sure you had everything you needed. That was how we showed love."

"Yes, Mama, I was provided for. But kids need more than just things. They need to know they're loved. They need to feel good about themselves and their accomplishments. They need to be encouraged to pursue their dreams, not shot down at every turn. I can honestly say I've never felt that – not in my entire life."

"Oh, honey, I never realized you felt like that. I always wanted what was best for you, but I was practical too. Yes, I've been proud of your going to school and your work. I just wish we could be closer and talk about these things."

"I'll tell you what, Mom. I'll try to be more conversational if you won't be so critical all the time. I do appreciate your help. If you want to be helpful, just offer! Telling me how to do something is not the same thing – it makes me feel like you don't approve of how I do whatever it is."

"All right, honey. I'll try, too. Forgive me for the hurt I've caused; I never knew you felt that way. I do love you and have always been proud of you."

"Thank you, Mama. I know I'm not sweet-natured, but I will try harder. I just get so preoccupied with everything. You're my mother, and I do love you, and I do want you here. You will always have a home with us."

That evening marked at least a little bit of a turning point for us. I tried to be nicer, and you were trying too. It wasn't always perfect after that, but we did achieve a type of civil détente and weren't on edge all the time. It's a good thing. As the next few years went by and my health declined, I realized more than ever how fortunate I was to have a home with you and Joe and the boys. I'm sure I don't tell you enough. What would I have done if you hadn't been here to call the ambulance when I couldn't breathe or take care of me after that heart surgery? I never want to be a burden, but I am grateful.

I'm so glad that we have at least some sense of a closer relationship these days. I guess we've both been more tolerant of each other. I don't know that I will have many more years with you, Joe, and the boys. Please know that I love you all. You will always be my baby girl –

Love,

Your Mother

MY REFLECTION FOUR

I wasn't sure what to think of this last set of letters. I would like to think they are true and sincere. I know many of the actual events are true – I remember well the night Mother asked if I wanted her to move out. Our conversation did seem to bring somewhat of a truce. It wasn't long after that that she got so sick, so then there was no question of being accommodating and kind.

The reason I say I would like to think they were sincere is simple. I don't know that my mother ever truly realized the hurt and damage caused by some of her sharp comments and pseudo-abandonment. Granted, I made sharp comments myself, and until the night of the big cry, I hadn't realized how hurtful they came across. I believe I've craved attention and recognition my entire life due to the lack of such during childhood.

Some of those statements ring in my ears after all this time. I can hear them as clearly as if she were speaking to me today. Although she said in one of the letters that she wished she could take it back, the one I can never forget is when she said, "People like us don't get to be things like that. You can be a teacher or a nurse." The funny thing is, I ended up becoming both of those! Looking back, I can see now that it should have been affirming. Both of those would require higher education, and no one in our family had ever pursued that. Albeit common choices for women in those days, at least they meant something more than a secretary or housewife. My therapist helped me to consider that this was my mother's way of protecting me. I wasn't at risk of disappointment as long I played things safe and chose something conventional and more easily achieved than some of my more fanciful ideas.

It was revealing to read some of my own mother's innermost thoughts, even if they were only invented in the wishful thinking of my mind. I never really felt fear when Mike was in Vietnam. I don't know why; I suppose it was just immaturity. As a mother of sons now, and especially after losing one, I regret that I was not more compassionate. I was just too wrapped up in my teenage drama to think of anyone but myself. The same could be said when my mother nursed Daddy through his illnesses. As a child, I never considered the possibility he might die. I also remember Mama coming home from work dripping wet with sweat. I never considered what it was like to work at manual labor in a factory in the heat of the summer. As she said, that was her way of showing love; nothing needed to be expressed otherwise. Parents showed love by providing for their kids. The problem is, children don't understand that. All I knew was that you said I couldn't join the choir or you couldn't come to the PTA program. I know the provisions of things and experiences like vacations were invaluable. Still, they are never the same as a gentle hug, a word of praise, or a proud smile.

It may sound strange, but the thing I worried about the most was that my Mama and Daddy would divorce! Although among my circle of friends, most of the mothers did not work outside of the home. That didn't bother me. But the thought of divorce was terrifying! I didn't really know anyone who lived in such a situation, so I don't know why it was so scary to me. I would lie in bed at night and hear my mother yelling at my daddy. I always felt sorry for him because it sounded like she was always the one doing the yelling. That was something we never discussed. I do know from how she took care of him at the end when he was sick and a few things she said after he died that she did love him. That has been reassuring. I hope and pray that he knew that, too.

So, life goes on. There are no more letters in the letter box - yet. My mother has been gone for over twenty-five years, and I have no daughters to reproach me or sling accusations. I'm sure my sons could do their fair share, but this book is about mothers and daughters, and now, granddaughters. The following letters will be added to the box.

Flagler Beach, Florida
February 2025

My Dearest Granddaughters,

There is so much I want to tell you! I hope these letters are not too rambling. I'm trying to organize these thoughts in some way that makes sense. First, I hope you learn from these women who have come before you. Each had their strengths and faults. Although it can be difficult not to judge or blame, that is not our responsibility. Who knows how any of us would have behaved in the same circumstances?

From Adeline, your fourth great-grandmother, there is much to learn. I think one of the most important lessons from her is to know that you can go from everything to nothing in the blink of an eye and still live a long and fruitful life.

From Harriet, your third great-grandmother, I hope you learn that holding grudges only takes up room in your heart that could be used to repair hurts and wounds. And it's never too late to reconnect and try to surmount life's disappointments.

From Tommie Belle, your second great-grandmother, I believe the lesson to be learned is to never desert those you love. No matter how difficult her life was, how hard she worked, or how many struggles she had to overcome, she promised to be there for her children. She upheld that promise until her death.

From your great-grandmother Mary, you could learn that abandonment isn't always physical. You can also learn that no parents are perfect, and it's so important to communicate with your children. My mother may have learned this by herself eventually, but our relationship could have been so different if she had realized it earlier.

And from me, your grandmother? What I hope you learn is that I love you all unconditionally. I know that, at times, I'm like my own mother.

I'm not always very good at expressing my feelings and showing my affection. Above all, what I want you to know is that I love each and every one of you. You are all beautiful and special and have so much potential. Each of you has your own gifts. That is my priority, that you know you are loved – no matter what – but there is much more I'd like to share with you.

Love you always,

Mahi

Flagler Beach, Florida
February 2025

Dear Girls and Young Ladies,

There is one word of wisdom I especially want you to know, mostly because it was denied to me. You can be whatever you want if you're willing to work for it. This is not just for women but for anyone. I always told your fathers and Uncle Jay this when they were young. It may not be easy, and at times, there may seem insurmountable odds against your dreams.

Remember back in the other letters when my mother said, "People like us don't get to be things like that."? Don't ever let anyone tell you that. Don't ever let anyone say you're not good enough or you can't become whatever you wish. Who are people like us anyway? If you've read these letters, then you know you come from a long line of hardworking, determined, strong women. That's who people like us are!

Don't be terribly disappointed if you discover what you thought you wanted to be doesn't work out. Live and learn. Our desires change, our circumstances change, our lives change. It may be that what you want to be at fifteen is different from what you want to be at twenty-five, thirty-five, or even seventy-five! I should know – I'm there, and I've worn many hats over the years. I'm not sorry for any of them; each has played a part in making me who I am. Who knows? There may be even more hats in my future.

Most importantly, remember that although you are a primary decision-maker, another entity is at play in your life. Each of you is a child of God. He will guide you if you let him. Pray for him to lead you on the path that you should go. You may take the wrong path at times, but there is no shame in that. There were times I wanted something so badly and just knew it was meant to be, but God closed the doors. Return to him and let him correct your direction. He may lead you on different paths at various times in your life, but he will never lead you astray. His words assure us. "'For I know the plans I have for you,' declares the Lord, 'plans to prosper you and not to harm you, plans to give you hope and a future.'" – Jeremiah 29:11.

I look forward to seeing where God leads each of you. I have every confidence each of you will be successful in determining and fulfilling God's will for your lives.

Love always,

Mahi

Flagler Beach, Florida
February 2025

Dear Granddaughters,

It's almost too late for this advice for one of you (wink wink), but I'm going to give it anyway. I know how much you all loved your dear PapaJoe. He was truly an incredible man. Not perfect, but amazingly, providentially, and divinely perfect for me. I know without any doubt that he was sent by God to be my mate for life, the father of my children, and grandfather of all of you.

That's not to say I was always that sure. That's why I want to share our love story with you. I was only eighteen when we started dating, and PapaJoe was twenty-seven. I know that sounds incredibly young and like a very wide age difference, but there were extenuating circumstances – I was already about to graduate college, and things were different in those days. I'd had a couple of what I thought at the time were serious relationships, but for one reason or another, they didn't work out. As we dated, I came to realize that Joe was a man – not a boy! I was convinced he was the man for me.

Why would I say I wasn't always so sure? It was only after we were married that I learned things about him I never knew before. Oh, we had the requisite pre-marital conference with our pastor. All I remember about it is him asking us about being Christians, wanting to have a Christian home, if we wanted children, and would we set good examples for them. No real "let's get to the practical details of life questions."

You never really know someone until you live with them. Trivial things can be overcome easily – how to squeeze the toothpaste tube, which way to hang the toilet paper. Other issues are not solved so effortlessly. Things I did not know when I married your PapaJoe? Here are just a few examples. He wanted to tell me what to wear. He did not want me to go to the apartment swimming pool without him. He did not want me to know how much money he made. He did not want me to have my own money – I had to ask for money from him. Sound surprising? It was surely surprising to me!

After a while, I began to resent these restraints. There was a time when I wasn't sure if I wanted to be married anymore! We went to a marriage counselor at our church. He led us through discovering what the issue really was. Joe had essentially married a girl with no frame of reference for what it meant to be married. The girl had grown up! Poor Joe had to deal with the fact he was now married to an opinionated, independent woman who wasn't going to be told what to do. He may have seemed grown and mature, but he had a lot of learning to do, as I did. We worked through things, and you know the result – over fifty years of a solid marriage.

All of this is to say, choose your mate in life carefully. There will be stars in your eyes, but don't let them blind you. Talk about the important things. How will big decisions be made? How will finances be handled? How does he feel about you working outside the home? Does he expect to control family decisions? Are you both willing to compromise on some issues? What are absolute non-negotiables? Infidelity? Abuse or violence? Irresponsible spending? Alcohol or drug abuse?

All marriages go through difficulties. That's to be expected. After all, look at what your several times great-grandmothers went through. Hopefully, you will have one other thing in your favor. God. He has already chosen a mate for you, and if you both put him first in your life, he will guide you through the fire. It doesn't mean life will be perfect. God knows there are plenty of "church people" in horrendous marriages. Pray for his guidance and ask yourself the hard questions before you make a commitment to anyone.

Well, I suppose that is enough preaching for now. There's still more to tell regarding some of life's hardest experiences.

I love you all and wish for your happiness,

Mahi

Flagler Beach, Florida
February 2025

Dear Darlings,

There is one thing in life you can count on for sure – change is inevitable. You may think, "Oh, I'll never get in a situation like that," or "My husband will always support me and our family," or "My children will never do such a thing!" I'm here to tell you that no matter what you believe will happen, there will be unexpected turns in events.

You will think you've gotten over a hurdle – searching for a new job, moving into a new home, buying a new vehicle, or getting pregnant. But then something goes wrong. The job doesn't turn out to be what you thought, the house contract falls through, the new cars are not in your budget, or there are complications with pregnancy.

The important thing is to go through life's troubles together. Men are often reticent to talk about their feelings. You don't have to push it, but make yourself available and stay attuned to their feelings. The same should be said of them for you. Let them know how you feel. Sometimes, a wife or mother will want to be the strong one, holding everything together while she is coming apart at the seams. That's not healthy.

I am fully convinced those stressful times contributed to my autoimmune conditions. Y'all don't know about the times PapaJoe had to work out of town during the Eastern Airlines strikes. I was basically a single parent trying to get three little boys to all their activities, work a demanding supposedly part-time job at church, and my mother living with us during this time. If you've read those letters, you know how difficult that could be at times. Then, when Eastern went bankrupt, PapaJoe was completely unemployed. That was a tough time financially. I got sick of answering the phone to bill collectors!

As hard as that was, it wasn't the toughest thing we endured. We went through PapaJoe going to school and eventually finding new employment with Delta. In the meantime, I determined I never wanted to be in such a precarious financial position again. I needed to be able to contribute to the support of our family, and part-time jobs were not going to hack it. That's when I decided to go back to school full-time and get my teaching certificate so I could be gainfully employed. All of that was stressful beyond words.

Life will pull the rug out from under you when you least expect it. Take care of each other. Support each other. Seek help if you need to, either for yourself or together as a couple. I spent several years working with a therapist, and it helped me beyond measure. Do what you must do to provide for your mate and your children, but not at the expense of your own sanity. You won't be doing anyone any favors if you distance yourself emotionally as my own mother did.

I love you all and pray your lives will not bring too much heartache. But you can be sure there will be some. You can face troubles with strength like your great-grandmothers did and with your faith in God.
Also, know that if I am still around, I will be here for you.

Love forever,

Mahi

Flagler Beach, Florida
February 2025

My Dearest Darlings,

The last thoughts I'd like to leave you with are these: Live life fully, pursue your dreams, and never take a moment for granted. None of us are guaranteed another day, another hour, or another moment. I have to say this is the biggest lesson I have learned in my life.

I spent far too much time worrying and working to make things right. Of course, I wanted the best for my family, but I wanted other things, too, things that were impossible to achieve. I wanted to create the perfect pediatric physician's job, but it was not to be. Time and circumstances were not ready for PAs in the early 1970s. I wanted to maintain the perfect educational environment for young children at Suzuki International Learning Center, but that did not jive with their desire to become a profitable daycare operation. I wanted to develop and manage a stellar Christian education preschool, but the authorities did not share that vision, so it didn't happen. I wanted to be a teacher who inspired and led other teachers, but my convictions and doggedness could not flourish within the system. All that time, the struggles were eating away at my health and peace of mind. It's a trite platitude that holds true: Sometimes, you must let go and let God.

This ultimate lesson was tragically imprinted on me when we lost Uncle Jay in 2009. One never expects to lose a child. Parents aren't supposed to outlive their children. That event, more than any other in my life, proved to me that life is so very fragile, and we never know when it will be snatched away. I believe had I not lived through losing Jay, it would have been even more of a shock losing PapaJoe the way I did.

After Jay died, I didn't want to live. Truly. I prayed not to wake up in the mornings. I wanted to become a drunk or drug addict so I did not have to face each day. But deep down inside, I knew PapaJoe needed me, although he never opened up about Jay's death. I knew your daddies needed me. And just think, like Jay, I never would have known any of you except for McKenzie and Macie. How tragic would that have been! Somehow, God pulled me through.

Then, suddenly, PapaJoe was gone. No warning, no inclination, not even the slightest whisper of suspicion. Vanished in the blink of an eye. But PapaJoe was seventy-seven, not twenty-eight. PapaJoe had lived a full life; Jay was about to be married and start a family. PapaJoe had retired from a lifetime of productive work. Jay was just realizing his dreams of being a teacher and coach. Not that it has made anything easier, but there's something so much more tragic about losing a young person.

Remarkably and unexpectedly, it was losing PapaJoe that made it possible for me to fulfill a lifelong dream of living on the beach. Not that it can ever replace love or people, and oh, how I wish PapaJoe and I could have done this together, but I never could convince him. I know he would be happy for me, and I have not regretted my move for a single minute.

Give the blessing in life, and you will be blessed. Not all of us are fortunate enough to receive the blessing. I think that was the case for some of these ancestors. The blessing is the giving of unconditional love through five elements. Meaningful touch is the showing of appropriate physical affection. Spoken words are verbal affirmations and expressions of love. Recognizing and attaching high value to a person's worth is another. Picturing and communicating positive futures are another. The final element of the blessing is a genuine commitment to demonstrating steadfast and unwavering support. To learn more about The Blessing, see The Blessing: Giving the Gift of Unconditional Love and Acceptance Paperback – June 4, 2019, by John Trent (Author), Gary Smalley (Author), and Kari Trent Stageberg (Author).

I hope and pray that each of you does not have to wait a lifetime to fulfill your dreams. Some of your dreams will come true sooner than others, and that is how it should be. I know young people are not always interested in the past, but I hope you can find wisdom and knowledge

from your ancestors, as I have done.
Know that I love and bless you.

Yours forever,

Mahi

BOOK CLUB DISCUSSION GUIDE

1 The first woman depicted in The Letter Box is Adeline. She lived a long life, born before the Civil War, and didn't die until 1936. What are some of the changes she saw in her lifetime? Do you think it was more or less challenging for women to cope with the difficulties of living in her time? Would it be different if a mother and father left their children in present times? From reading her letters, what were her strengths and weaknesses? What do you believe the legacy is that Adeline left to her descendants?

2. The second woman, Adeline's daughter Harriet, never overcame her resentment towards her mother. Do you feel this resentment is justified? Should she have forgiven her mother? Why or why not? Do you believe it is possible to overcome such strong feelings that are endured early in life? How? Although Harriet's abandonment of her own daughter was after Tommie Belle was grown, how was it the same or different from her own abandonment? What do you believe the legacy is that Harriet left to her descendants?

3. It appears that Tommie Belle, the third mother, begins to break the pattern of abandonment. How is her determination not to repeat this pattern evident? Is she justified in feeling her own mother, Harriet, abandoned her even though she was grown? How do Tommie Belle's life circumstances, so different from her mother's and grandmother's, affect her attitudes toward her daughters? What do you believe the legacy is that Harriet left to her descendants?

4. How is Mary, the fourth mother, different from her ancestors? What events in her life shaped

her? How was her abandonment of her younger children different from Adeline's and Harriet's abandonment of their daughters? Was the emotional abandonment justified by Mary's life circumstances? Do you believe people recognize this type of abandonment as legitimate?

5. How was Mary's life, nearly a hundred years in the future of her own grandmother, different from her forebears? What do you believe Mary's legacy is for her descendants?

6. How do Janet's, the fifth mother, reflections reveal her feelings about her ancestors? How has this influenced her life? How could it have affected her role as a mother to sons instead of daughters? Are Janet's feelings about her mother, Mary, justified? How do the different times of her life affect what she has gained from learning about her ancestors? What legacy do you think Janet wants to leave for her granddaughters?

7. Some Mother /daughter relationships are fraught with difficulty, while others seem almost idyllic. Why do you think this is? How does either type of relationship affect those involved? How can it affect the legacy left for their descendants?

8. Although the fathers in the lives of these women are not explored in depth, what role do you think they could have played? Could they have made a difference in the daughters' perceptions of their mothers? How important are fathers in mother/daughter relationships? Is a father's connection to his daughter as crucial as that of a mother? How do father/daughter and mother/daughter bonds differ? How are they alike?

The Letter Box

The Letter Box

www.ingramcontent.com/pod-product-compliance
Lightning Source LLC
Chambersburg PA
CBHW030600310726
48979CB00003B/519

* 9 7 8 1 9 5 3 4 1 6 3 1 5 *